Spilling the Spice

A Spicetown Mystery

Sheri Richey

Sheri Richey

Copyright © 2019 Sheri S. Richey. All rights reserved. No part of this book may be reproduced or transmitted in any form or by any means, electronic or mechanical, including photocopying, recording or by an information storage or retrieval system now known or hereto after invented—except by a reviewer who may quote brief passages in a review to be printed in a magazine or newspaper—without permission in writing from the publisher.

For further information, contact the publisher: Amazon Publishing.

The author assumes no responsibility for errors or omissions that are inadvertent or inaccurate. This is a work of fiction and is not intended to reflect actual events or persons.

ISBN: 978-1-64633-598-5

Cover art by Mariah Sinclair

Spicetown Mysteries

Welcome to Spicetown
A Bell in the Garden
Spilling the Spice
Blue Collar Bluff
A Tough Nut to Crack

Chapter 1

"I'm almost finished with Paprika Parkway," Amanda Morgan said when she met Mayor Bingham at the corner of Fennel and Clove Street. "I just have these four businesses to go."

"Here," Cora Mae said, reaching for the stack of fliers that Amanda was carrying. "I'll take some and go down Ginger Street. I can drop them off at the businesses there as I'm walking to the Sweet & Sour Spice Shop."

"Okay," Amanda said waving as she turned to cross the street. "I'll see you back at City Hall."

Cora rearranged the pages she was carrying. Her assistant, Amanda, had created some eye-catching graphics for the parade and all the Spicetown Fourth of July festivities. She really had a knack for graphic design.

"Hello, Saucy," Cora said in surprise when she turned to see her old friend, Harvey Salzman, walking across the street toward her. "Out for a walk today?"

"Morning, Mayor. It's a beautiful day. Can I help you carry those?"

"Thank you, Saucy, but I've got them. You might want one though," Cora said handing him a flier. "I'm just going to drop these off at stores on Ginger Street."

"So, the statue unveiling is after the parade?"

"Yes, I'm hoping once the parade is over, everyone will move towards the craft fair and carnival so it will be a good central meeting point to do the reveal."

"I saw the article in the paper," Saucy said as he tapped his finger on the picture of John Spicer. "It's really exciting that you found some of his ancestors."

"Yes, I haven't met them yet, but they are arriving tomorrow night and they're going to ride with me in the parade. The statute turned out really well. I can't wait for everyone to see it."

"I will try to be there," Saucy said with a grimace, "But I really don't like big crowds."

"Oh, you have to come," Cora said squeezing his arm. "There will be something for everyone and it'll be so much fun. I love a parade."

"I'm going in Peppercorn Cleaners. Do you want me to take a stack of fliers to them?"

"Yes, that would be a big help. Thank you." Cora handed Saucy a small stack and waved as he crossed the street to go into the dry cleaners. As she approached the Sweet & Sour Spice Shop, Cora spied Police Chief Conrad Harris on the sidewalk with both fists planted at his waist staring at the cluster of motorcycles gathered outside.

"Are you thinking of taking up a dangerous hobby?" Cora Mae snickered as Conrad scowled at her remark.

"I was wondering if we were on the map for a poker run. You don't often see so many bikes in Spicetown all at one time. Are you planning to go in there?" Conrad pointed to the Sweet & Sour Spice Shop and lifted one eyebrow.

"I am," Cora said lifting her chin. "I'm dropping off some fliers and I need to speak to Karen Goldman for a minute if she's--."

Before Cora could complete her sentence, they both heard a loud crash from inside the store. Squeals of surprise from startled patrons soon followed the sound of breaking glass. Cora pushed past Conrad to get to the door.

"Why don't you wait—?" Conrad tried to stall Cora's entry until he could determine the cause of the noise but scurried after her when she threw open the door and ignored his comment.

The cause was immediately apparent as a long table holding spice samples had toppled to its side and dozens of glass spice jars were broken. A large man was splayed in the center of broken glass and a kaleidoscope of colorful spices were splashed across the floor. The already pungent odor of the shop was almost unbearable as the strong aromas mixed together and several shoppers drifted outdoors to escape the smell.

"Sorry. Sorry, I've made a mess. Don't worry," the man said standing and brushing spice powder from the legs of his trousers. "I'll pay for it. I'll reimburse you for everything."

Karen Goldman, the manager of the Sweet & Sour Spice Shop, reached her hand out to help the man stand as a young woman with purple tinged hair fluttered around him, brushing off his back.

"Are you okay?" Karen looked him over carefully through squinted eyes. "Are you cut anywhere?"

"Oh, he's fine," the young woman said with a dismissive wave to Karen as she continued brushing off the back of his legs with her hand."

"Yeah, I'm okay," he said stepping gingerly through the broken glass. "Here," he said reaching in his back pocket and then patting his front pockets. "Linda, where's my wallet?"

"I guess you left it in the room," she said shrugging.

"Here's my card," he said handing Karen Goldman a business card from his shirt pocket. "I'm Booze Lockhart and I'm staying right over there at the Nutmeg Inn. I'll pay for all your damages. Don't you worry."

"Oh, okay," Karen said stammering as she perused the damage before glancing at the business card.

"Just write me up a bill and send it over to the inn. I'll take care of it."

"Come on, baby. Let's go," the young woman said as she tugged on the crook of Booze's elbow. "You need to get out of her way so she can clean up your mess. Really, I don't know what's gotten into you lately."

"Okay, okay. I'm going. Again, real sorry, honey," Booze said to Karen Goldman as she approached them with her broom in her hand. Karen ignored his comment and began sweeping up cumin powder and oregano that had blended into a powerful combination.

As the motorcyclist departed at the sight of Conrad Harris' entrance, Cora rushed over to Karen. "Is everything okay? What happened?"

"Hi, Mayor. Yes, everything is okay, I guess," Karen said with an exhausted huff. "It's been so busy with all these people in and out. It's just crazy. The town celebration has brought in a lot of visitors."

"Well, I hope it's brought you a lot of sales, too," Cora said patting Karen's back as she swept.

"Not really," Karen said frowning. "I feel like I'm running a museum. Everyone wants to look and touch, but not many sales. And now this," Karen said sweeping her hand out over the damage.

"What happened here?" Conrad said over the roar of motorcycles all pulling onto the street at once. "Was this guy part of the motorcycle group?"

"No, I don't think so, but maybe… He did seem to know one of them and they wore jackets that said Buckeyes on the back. I don't know what happened. He just appeared to fall over without warning and grabbed the table when he fell."

"Oh, dear. What a mess. I heard him tell you he plans to pay for it, at least." Cora picked up the plastic wastebasket near the cash register and brought it over near the spill. "Don't you have any help today?"

"Darlene is scheduled. She should be here real soon."

"Karen, do you usually draw motorcycle enthusiasts?" Conrad frowned as Cora rolled her eyes at him.

"He's obsessed with all the bikes out front," Cora said as Karen chuckled.

"No, Chief. This was the first time. One of them did buy something though, some barbecue spice rub. Maybe they're planning a cookout for the holiday."

"Maybe," Conrad said stroking his chin. "So, what was this guy's story?"

"I've seen him here before." Karen lifted the dust pan and emptied its contents into the wastebasket. "He said he was staying at the Nutmeg Inn, but I thought he was living here because he's come in several times."

"I hope you send him a bill." Cora picked up a few spice bottles that had rolled across the room without breaking. "You've lost at least eight jars of spice here and one of them is your famous homemade blend of pumpkin spice."

"I'll have to ask Ned first. I think he knows this guy and he may not want me to bill him."

"Ned Carey knows this guy?" Conrad snapped to attention and straightened his posture. "How do you know?"

"The guy has asked for Ned before when he's been in. He acted like he knew Ned and obviously he knew Ned owned the store. That's why I remember him. Well, that and he always calls me honey or sweetie. Ugh. I can't stand that." Karen shuddered and shook her head.

"Hmm," Conrad hummed as Cora reached for the business card Karen had left on the counter.

"Booze Lockhart, Red River Ranch," Cora handed the card to Conrad.

"Maybe Ned did some legal work for him. Red River is not very far up the road. I'm surprised he would get a room at the inn." Conrad discreetly pulled out his phone and took a photo of the business card as Cora gave him a quizzical look.

"I'm sure he just doesn't want to miss the parade," Cora said with her excitement bubbling out. "That's actually why I'm here. I brought you some fliers to leave by the register. It has all the times listed for the events and it shows the parade route. It's coming right by the store. Are you riding on your float?"

"I don't think so," Karen said as she tied a knot in the trash bag and pulled it out of the wastebasket. Conrad moved to help Karen set up the table again as Cora collected some of the undamaged items to put back on the tabletop. "I think Darlene may ride with Ned and I'm going to stay in the store that day. I can catch a glimpse as it goes by and when Darlene gets back, I'll go check out the craft fair."

"I don't want you to miss it. It's going to be a great event." Cora snapped her fingers. "Oh, and I need some Darjeeling Tea. Do you still have some or did Mr. Lockhart break that, too?"

§

Walking back to City Hall, Cora couldn't resist nudging into Conrad's deep concentration. "So, what do you think about this Lockhart guy?"

"It's odd," Conrad frowned and glanced over at Cora. "The pieces don't fit together. This guy falls over suddenly and then seems fine. He stays at Nutmeg Inn but claims to live on Red River Ranch. He speaks to the bikers like he knows them and asks for Ned Carey, our city attorney. I've never seen him before, but Karen says he's visited several times. Something's off."

"Now, this can all be explained away easily," Cora said playing devil's advocate. "He could just come to town for the spice occasionally but wanted to stay this time for the fireworks. He might have been talking with the bikers because he's a gregarious type of guy. He may not even know them personally. You know, some people just chat with you when you shop, and they are complete strangers. I do it all the time."

"And the fall?" Conrad raised an eyebrow in disbelief.

"He could have dizzy spells. Maybe he has a medical condition." Cora wished she could sound more convincing because it all seemed odd to her, too.

"I'm going to ask Ned about it at coffee tomorrow morning." Conrad always met the regulars down at the Fennel Street Bakery for coffee each day. Ned Carey was usually among them.

"Good idea," Cora nodded as they reached Paprika Parkway. "Can you drop these off at Sesame Subs on your way back to the station?"

"Sure," Conrad said as Cora straightened her stack of remaining fliers.

"Who are you going to put in the lead car and the last car in the parade?"

"I'm going to drive the lead car and let Roy Asher bring up the tail. Wink is going to walk along the perimeter with Tabor. Did the sheriff confirm?"

"He did and I told him he'd be behind you. He didn't seem to have a problem with that."

"You know, Cora, I don't care about those things. If Bobby Bell wants to be the first car, I am fine with that."

"Well, I'm not," Cora huffed. "This is Spicetown's parade and our police chief should be first. The sheriff will be fine following."

"He may not show up if you've bruised his ego. He may send a deputy instead."

"All the better," Cora smiled. "I won't have time for his ego. Will Wink be able to stay awake? Doesn't he always work nights? I thought you'd use Sammy."

"I'm giving Georgia the day off because she's doing something with the craft fair and Sammy is going to be on dispatch. Wink actually asked to come. He wants to bring his dog, Hank, with him."

"Tell him that's fine. I don't mind but Hank has to be on a leash. How is the new guy?" Cora smiled when Conrad looked away in search of a response.

"He's trying." Conrad shrugged and looked down at Cora. "He's young yet. If Roy doesn't corrupt him totally, he might do okay."

"Mrs. Bing. Mrs. Bing!" Cora snapped to attention and searched the street for the voice. Seeing Nellie Turner across the street waving one hand over her head and clutching her camera with the other, Cora waved back.

"Oh, no," Conrad muttered softly. "I'll take these to the sub shop and see you later." Conrad tried to snatch the fliers from Cora, but she kept her hand firmly planted over them as Nellie ran across the street with the small camera around her neck bouncing against her chest.

"Good morning, Miss Nellie. How are you today?" Cora smiled kindly at Nellie Turner as Conrad shifted to stand behind Cora, looking down the street longingly.

"It's a wonderful day, Mrs. Bing. I'm so lucky I caught you and Chief Harris together. Can I take your picture?"

"Certainly, Nellie. Go right ahead." Cora stepped sideways to put Conrad next to her and ignored his groaning objections.

"Now, Miss Nellie, you know I don't like my picture taken," Conrad said as he shuffled his feet to avoid posing.

"I know, Chief, but I promise it doesn't hurt at all," Nellie said sincerely. "I let Tommy take my picture all the time and I can't even tell when he does it."

Nellie held up the camera and peered at them for a second, but Cora didn't even hear a click. With a quick jerk, Nellie waved goodbye to them and ran back across the street to where her brother, Tommy, stood waiting for her.

"Have a good day," Cora called out waving to them both as Tommy waved back shyly.

"Why do you indulge her?" Conrad shook his head in disappointment.

"Why do you resist?" Cora countered with a sharp shrug of her shoulders. "She's harmless and she enjoys it."

"I don't like pictures," Conrad grumbled.

"She doesn't have any film in there," Cora scoffed. "It makes her happy and it's a little thing. You should just go with the flow, Connie."

"How do you know she doesn't?"

"She can't possibly afford it. Nellie and Tommy are barely scraping by day to day. If their mother hadn't owned that old house out on Rosemary Road, they'd be homeless. They get by on the day-old bread from Fennel Street Bakery and handouts from the kind citizens of Spicetown. She's just passing time walking through town and taking pictures with an empty camera. Indulge her next time."

Conrad groaned and reached for the fliers again. "I'll drop these off for you. Do I need to tell them anything?"

"Tell them I'll be looking for their smiling faces at the parade," Cora said laughing at Conrad's scowl as they parted company and she headed back to City Hall.

§

"I'm back," Cora called out in a sing-song voice as she walked in Amanda's office door. "Mission accomplished."

"Good," Amanda said following Cora through her office and leaning on the door frame of Cora's office door waiting for her to get settled at her desk. "I have some bad news."

"Oh, no. That's not allowed," Cora snapped. "We are too close to launch day. What's happened?"

"Well, Councilman Langley has been by and wants to see you. He insists that his daughter ride with you in the parade because he is not available. He feels he is entitled to be there because he is the most senior member on the City Council."

"I'll talk to him," Cora muttered and shook her head. "That's not so bad."

"That's not all," Amanda said with a sigh. "We've lost one of the VFW color guards. Mr. Johnson was hospitalized last night. They are looking for a replacement now."

"Oh, goodness. I hope he's all right. Perhaps they could contact the chapter in Paxton for a replacement for him."

"We've lost two of the riders for the horses at the end of the parade, too."

"Make a call to your dad and see if he knows anyone who is a good rider," Cora said. "Isn't he the vet for all the farms in the area? He'll know who to ask."

"Yes," Amanda said shaking her head. "I should have thought of that. Did we get confirmation back from the scouts?"

"Yes, they are going right behind the high school band and they are walking together. If the girls want to get on one side and the boys on the other, that's fine with me, but I'm not going to have any bickering about who goes first."

"Good," Amanda said marking that off her list. "Rodney Maddox has the equipment now to record everything. He borrowed it and tested it all out. He's going to set up next door to City Hall so he can video your statue dedication too."

"Fantastic," Cora cheered. "You know, I saw a group of motorcycles today in front of the Sweet & Sour

Spice Shop. I think they are a part of a club called the Buckeyes. They left before I got a chance to talk to them, but that would be an interesting entry in the parade. Make a note to find out about them, would you? We should invite them. So, your bad news was not really so bad."

"Oh, and the last thing," Amanda said holding up a finger. "Councilman Langley wants to say a few words at the statue dedication after you—."

"Ab-so-lutely not!" Cora Mae slapped her hand down on her desk and growled. "They tried to stop me every step of the way and Larry was leading them on. He is not going to get up there and try to take credit for all the hard work we did to get that statue up there. In fact, I plan to tell the whole town exactly how the dedication came to be and include the unwillingness and downright refusal of the council to support my vision. He's not getting anywhere near that stage."

"Okay, okay. I'll just let you tell him that…" Amanda smiled and backed slowly out of Cora's doorway holding her hand up defensively in front of her.

"That man," Cora growled again as Amanda disappeared. Grabbing the phone, Cora called Jimmy Kole into her office to go over some details about the craft fair and took a deep calming breath. She had planned to invite Larry Langley's daughter to ride with her, but his last request had put her off that idea.

Sheri Richey

Chapter 2

"Georgie," Conrad called out as he saw Georgia Marks walk by his office door.

"Yeah, Chief?"

"Just wanted to let you know I changed the schedule. I switched Wink and Reynolds for a couple of days so Wink can be in the parade."

"You're putting Adam Reynolds on tonight's shift?" Georgia's eyes widened.

"Yeah," Conrad said. "He'll be fine. It's a weeknight. Nothing going on."

"Chief, the town is full of visitors roaming around. Are you sure?"

"I'll keep an eye on him." Conrad glared at Georgia until she shrugged and moved down the hallway to the dispatch cubicle just as his phone rang.

"Hey, Connie," Cora chirped. "I just heard from the Spicers and they will be here in an hour. I'm going to take them to dinner. Do you want to join us?"

"Sure. Where are you taking them?"

"I just made a reservation at the Barberry Tower. I invited Amanda and Bryan to come along since Amanda has talked to them. She's the one that found them for me."

"Okay," Conrad said glancing at the time on his computer. "Do you want me to meet you there or pick you up?"

"I have to meet them at the Nutmeg Inn."

"I'll just pick you up and we'll go get them. Okay?" Conrad clicked his computer to shut down. He had just enough time to shower and change into street clothes.

"Okay. See you soon."

§

Conrad pulled his car into the driveway at Cora's house and was concerned when he pulled all the way up to her door without her head popping out. She always ran out the door at the first sign of his car. He only honked to aggravate her, but this time he hesitated. If she really was delayed, he didn't want to show impatience, so he let the car idle. After only a few seconds, he saw her look out from behind the kitchen curtains and then she hurried out the side door.

"I didn't know you were out here," Cora said breathlessly as she slid into the front seat and pushed her handbag down beside her feet. "You should have honked."

"You always scold me when I honk," Conrad said chuckling.

"That's because you only do it when you see I'm coming out of the door. *This* was one of those times when you were supposed to honk," Cora said slapping Conrad's arm with the back of her hand. "Silly."

Conrad laughed and shook his head. "I just can't seem to get that right."

"Gretchen just called me and said the Spicers are all checked in the Nutmeg Inn. I told her to let them know we are on our way to pick them up. They brought their grandson with them, too. Gretchen said he was a sweet boy, young teen she said, and he's excited about the parade. My kind of kid!" Cora shook her fist in the air.

"You didn't know he was coming? Will you have room in the car?"

"Oh, yes. In fact, it works out perfectly. Larry Langley wanted his daughter to ride with me, but now he's made me mad, so I have the perfect reason to tell him, no. Now there isn't room for her."

Conrad nodded as he backed out of her driveway on Bay Leaf Boulevard and headed to Ginger Street. "Do these people know about John Spicer?"

"Amanda has communicated with them more than I have, but they know about him. Someone in the family is interested in genealogy so they know their family tree. Amanda said they knew their great grandfather was from Spicetown, but they didn't know that he was the first resident here or that they named the town for him. As it turns out, John is actually a family name that's passed down, so the man we're meeting is John Michael Spicer. He goes by Mike though."

"Interesting," Conrad murmured as he slowed his car in front of the Nutmeg Inn and parked on the street. As Cora gathered her purse from the floor, Conrad sent a quick text to Sam at dispatch to let him know where he was. Georgia's warning words about leaving the new officer to work a night alone kept echoing in his subconscious. Maybe this dinner hadn't been such a good idea. He was afraid Reynolds would need him and would have felt better if he had stayed in the station listening to the police radio.

Cora was already hugging Gretchen when Conrad entered the Nutmeg Inn and he waved to Gretchen's husband, Levi Nauchtman, when he came out of the backroom behind the check-in counter.

"Have you come to pick up the town celebrities?" Levi smiled and extended his hand to shake. "I told them they were the stars of the parade this year."

"I'm the official chauffeur," Conrad said shaking Levi's hand. "Just honored to be included."

"Well, that young man they brought with them is sure excited about the event. We don't get many young people through here, not near enough," Levi shook his head and put his hands in his pockets. "He's a pistol."

Gretchen chuckled as she slipped her hand through the crook of her husband's arm. "Yes, he's an excited young man. I bet he'll have a million questions for you at dinner."

"Cora's pretty excited about the parade, too," Conrad said smiling. "I'm sure they'll have a lot to talk about."

"Hey, darlin', can you hand me that backdoor key?" Gretchen jumped at the sound and reached under the counter to hand Booze Lockhart a key on a large wooden keyring that read Nutmeg Inn.

Booze didn't give Conrad or Cora any notice as he turned to walk down the hallway towards the rear of the house.

Gretchen looked up at Cora apologetically, but Cora waved her concern away. "We met Mr. Lockhart earlier today. Well," Cora glanced at Conrad slyly, "maybe met isn't the right word. We saw Mr. Lockhart earlier today when he knocked over a table in the Sweet & Sour Spice Shop. He made quite a mess, but he told Karen he was staying here."

"Yes, he's stayed here several times. Lives over in Red River but has business here in town. He goes out back to smoke about every few minutes." Conrad saw a sneer of disapproval on Levi's face as Gretchen explained.

"He lost his balance in the store and fell over," Conrad said looking at Levi. "Has he had any problem here?"

"I suspect he drinks a bit," Levi said winking. "He gets a little loud sometimes."

"Pushy," Gretchen muttered softly to Cora. "Oh, I hear your guests coming."

Cora looked up the stairway as a young man ran down the stairs with wide eyes and jumped to the floor to skip the last step. A gray-haired gentleman followed closely behind the young man cautioning him not to run, as a woman followed holding the stairway railing.

"Mr. Spicer?" Cora turned to face the family as they reached the lobby.

"That's me!" The young man jumped in front of Cora and extended his right hand as the elder Spicer clasped his wife's hand for the last step of the stairs. Both chuckled at the boy's boldness.

Conrad rocked back on his heels and laughed when Cora beamed at the boy. This was going to be an exciting dinner.

§

"You go on ahead," Conrad whispered to Cora as they entered the Barberry Tower. "I need to check in with the office."

Cora nodded and then began craning her neck around the restaurant looking for Amanda. "This way," Cora motioned to the Spicers to follow her to a long table where Bryan and Amanda were sitting.

"Mike," Cora said once they approached the table. "This is my assistant, Amanda Morgan. I believe you've spoken with her a number of times."

"Yes, I have. It's nice to finally meet you, Amanda. This is my wife, Ellen, and my grandson, Bradley."

"Wonderful," Amanda cooed as she shook Bradley's hand when he offered it to her. "This is my boyfriend, Bryan Stotlar."

Everyone finished their greetings and chose a chair as Cora glanced through the doorway looking for Conrad.

"Have you had a chance to tour Spicetown yet?" Bryan asked as he returned to his seat.

"We have a bit on our own," Mike Spicer said. "We've come through town before. Ellen likes the little craft shop on the corner, and we stopped in town one day when we were passing through."

"Oh, the Carom Seed Craft Corner?" Amanda said.

"Yes," Ellen Spicer said smiling. "I do a little quilting and they have some lovely fabrics in there."

"We will need one more chair," Cora whispered to the hostess while everyone settled into their seats at the long table. Bradley sat prominently at the head of the table next to Cora and leaned towards her.

"Mayor, can you tell me what you know about the railroad now?"

"Give us a minute, honey," Ellen Spicer said smiling. "Let's get our food ordered first. Okay?"

"Is everything okay?" Cora said when Conrad sat down across the table from her with a wry smile on his face.

"Yeah," Conrad grunted as he scooted in his chair, but his smile only broadened when he saw Cora's inquisitive stare. "The new kid. He got himself tangled up a little bit."

"Tangled up?" Cora sat up straight and frowned.

"He pulled over Miriam for speeding," Conrad tried to stifle his laughter, but a chortle escaped. Cora didn't even try to conceal her delight and giggled heartily.

"Miriam Landry is our Chamber of Commerce President," Cora explained to the Spicers. "She has a testy personality, to put it mildly." The Spicers smiled and nodded. "So, did she have a hissy fit?"

"Oh, yes," Conrad said releasing his laughter. "She threatened to do everything but tar and feather him. He gave her a ticket anyway, so I can't say he doesn't have guts."

"Well, good for him," Cora beamed. She couldn't help but take delight in Miriam's misery. The woman caused everyone else so much distress with her sour demeanor. "Let's order."

Chapter 3

The dinner went well, and Cora finally had her captive audience. She recited the history of Spicetown for the young Spicer and filled in the historical facts to all the questions his young mind could conjure.

"Bradley, you're wearing the mayor out now," Mike Spicer said apologetically. "He has a curious mind."

"Oh, she loves to talk about this stuff," Conrad said as he reached into his pocket when he felt his phone vibrate.

"Yes, no one wants to hear it," Cora said rolling her eyes at Conrad. "I have to pay Amanda to listen."

As everyone at the table laughed, Conrad slid from his seat without a word and walked to the entrance of the restaurant with his phone to his ear. Sam Crawford answered Conrad's call before it completed one ring.

"Chief, Reynolds needs you over at the Nutmeg Inn. There's a dead body in the back alley." Conrad had seen the 10-70 code on the text message before he called Sam, so he knew someone was dead. The code was a request to call the coroner.

"Who is it?"

"Don't know," Sam said, "but he's talking to the Nauchtmans about it now."

"Call the coroner and tell Reynolds I'm on my way." Conrad said a silent prayer that Adam Reynolds would remember his training and not mess up the scene.

"I'm sorry, folks," Conrad said as he approached the table. "I've got something urgent I need to get to, but I can send a car over to get everyone a ride back."

"That's okay, Chief," Brian said. "We can run them back to the Nutmeg Inn. We've got Amanda's SUV tonight. There's plenty of room."

"Great. Okay. Again, really sorry, but I've got to go. It was nice meeting all of you and I'll see you again at the parade."

"Nice to meet you, too, Chief," Mike Spicer said as his wife nodded her head. "It's perfectly okay. You go take care of business. We'll be fine here."

"I'm going with you," Cora muttered as she stood from her chair. "Amanda can't possible get us all in her car."

Conrad frowned but had to agree with Cora's assessment. He would drop her off as soon as the situation was under control. She could visit with the Nauchtmans while he checked out the alley. Conrad quickly paid the check for the table while Cora said her goodbyes and they rushed out the door.

"What's happened?" Cora asked as they opened the car doors. Conrad waited until they were inside the car to tell her about the call.

"But that's where the Spicers are going."

"I know, but hopefully the body will be gone before Bryan brings them back. It's in the back of the building off the alley, so they won't see anything. Maybe this is Sam," Conrad said as he felt his phone vibrate again.

Conrad put the phone back in his pocket without answering. "No. It's just Miriam," Conrad said with an exaggerated sigh. "I'm sure she wants to yell at me, but she'll have to wait."

"Did Sam give you any details? I mean, is the person injured or was there an accident?"

"Nothing, just dead. Reynolds didn't have any details yet. He was talking to the Nauchtmans."

Conrad pulled his car in the alley and parked behind Officer Reynolds' squad car. Cora's car door flew open before Conrad could get his seatbelt off. He knew it was useless to try to stop her.

Conrad quickly called dispatch to let Sam know he'd arrived as Reynolds approached the car. "Hey, Chief."

"Just talked to Sammy and the coroner is on the way."

"Good," Reynolds said nodding. "Hey Chief, do you know a Miss Nellie Turner?"

"Nellie!" Cora bolted around Officer Reynolds' police car and headed for the back door of the Nutmeg Inn.

"Is that who you found?" Conrad leaned around Reynolds to see where Cora had gone. "Cora, wait."

"Oh, no Chief. She wants to talk to you," Reynolds said as he followed Conrad toward the Inn.

"Geez, Reynolds. Who does the body belong to? Maybe you could lead with that."

"Oh, sorry Chief."

"It's Booze Lockhart," Cora said as Conrad reached the spot Cora was standing. The three stared down at the body sprawled on the side of the alley just a few feet from the back door of the Inn.

"It is, indeed," Conrad said with his hands at his waist. "And yes, I do know Miss Nellie. Why? Is she here?"

"She's inside, Chief. She said she needs to talk to you. Wouldn't say much else, but she's wound a little tight. Pretty anxious about something and won't talk to me."

"Cora, why don't you go inside and see if you can calm Miss Nellie." Cora nodded in agreement as she looked up and Conrad followed her gaze. A second-story window was right above the body.

"Reynolds, you need to get back on patrol. It sounds like Hudson can use your help," Conrad said pointing at the police radio on Reynolds' belt. A call had just come over the radio that Officer Hudson needed assistance at the Wasabi. Wasabi Women was a dance club on the edge of town that frequently attracted the wrong kind of tourist. The alcohol served could turn the slightest disagreement into a police call in an instant.

"Okay, Chief."

"The back door is locked," Cora said pulling on the handle and then knocking hard on the top pane.

"Yeah, it always locks when you shut it," Officer Reynolds said. "You have to have a key to get in."

"And write this scene up as soon as you're done at the Wasabi. I'll need your report tonight."

"Right, Chief. On my way." Reynolds pulled open his car door just as Levi Nauchtman opened the back door for Cora.

"Oh, and radio Sammy to send someone over with a camera." Conrad rarely drove his personal vehicle because as soon as he did, he needed all the equipment in his squad car.

Reynolds gave him a thumbs up sign as he drove by him and Conrad pulled a notebook from his shirt pocket. That was one tool he never left behind, and he began his notes with a sketch of the body's position.

Cora walked into the lobby of the inn and sat down beside Nellie Turner on the sofa. "Nellie, the Chief is really busy right now. Is there something I can do for you?"

"Oh, I have to talk to the Chief. I've got something really important to tell him."

"Well, he'll be inside shortly but he has things to take care of outside right now."

"Oh, I know there's a dead guy out there. That's what I need to talk to him about." Nellie was wringing her hands and sitting on the edge of her seat.

Cora glanced over at the counter when she heard someone walk out of the back room. "Gretchen? Could you get us some tea, please?" Cora darted her eyes over to Nellie and Gretchen nodded with a wary look.

"Certainly, Cora."

"Now Nellie, you don't want to get involved with all of this." Cora reached over to pat Nellie's wringing hands, but Nellie jumped up off of the sofa.

"Oh, I know Mrs. Bing. I can't help it though."

"Well, promise me you won't tell anybody else. You can tell the Chief whatever you need to, but don't talk to anyone else about this."

"Oh, no ma'am I won't talk to anyone, but the Chief. Can't I just go out there?"

"No Nellie, you need to stay inside. We'll have some tea."

"I've already seen the dead guy. He's just on the ground out there." Nellie pointed toward the back door.

"I know Nellie, but they have police things to do. You don't want to get in their way. Where is your brother, Tommy? He's usually with you."

"Oh, he was here, but he needed to get home. I told him I had to wait on the Chief, so he went ahead."

"Maybe it would be best if I call and get you a ride home. It's a long walk to do alone in the dark. Then the Chief can come by tomorrow and talk with you."

"Oh, no," Nellie said sitting back down again beside Cora. "I have to wait on him. This can't wait until tomorrow."

"Okay, Nellie," Cora said patting Nellie's clasped hands. "We'll just wait."

"Cora," Gretchen said with concern edging her voice. "I think someone's here. Out front." Gretchen pointed to the car lights and Cora peered over the top of the cafe curtains in the front window.

"Oh, I think it's Amanda. She's bringing back the Spicers." Cora frowned and looked at Gretchen. "I'd really rather they not know about all this."

"Definitely," Gretchen said running around the counter and over to Nellie. "Miss Nellie, can you come in the kitchen with me for a few minutes? I need to make some coffee for the Chief, and I could use your help."

"Sure," Nellie said popping up from her seat. "We need to make tea for Mrs. Bing. She likes tea the best."

"That's a great idea, Nellie. I'll go with you," Cora said scurrying behind Nellie to get out of the lobby before the Spicers entered. Gretchen stayed at the front desk to greet the Spicers and Cora led Nellie to the table.

"Let's see," Cora said looking around the room. "Let's start with the tea kettle. I see it's already on the stove. Can you fill the coffee pot about halfway with water? I'll see if I can find the coffee. Miss Gretchen will be here as soon as she takes care of her customers."

"Why do you think they killed that man, Mrs. Bing?"

"Oh, we don't know that someone killed him, Nellie. Maybe he was sick and just died out there."

"I don't think so, Mrs. Bing. You know, my Uncle Leo was sick, and he died, but he looked real sick. That man was okay last night because I talked to him and took his picture. He wasn't sick."

"Well, there are things that can happen really quick. Not everyone is sick for a long time like Uncle Leo."

"My momma was put in a hospital to die and Uncle Leo died at home. I don't think people just die in the alley. Somebody must have been really mad at him."

Cora jumped when she heard the knock on the back door and opened the side door of the kitchen to get access to the hall. She could see Conrad through the small glass window at the top of the door.

"The deputy coroner is here now so I'm going to get out of their way for a few minutes." Conrad followed Cora through the side door into the kitchen.

"We're making some coffee if you'd like some," Cora said as Conrad placed his camera on the kitchen counter.

"Oh, Chief," Nellie said jumping up from her seat at the table. "Can I talk to you?"

Conrad pulled out a chair and sat at the small table in the middle of the kitchen. "I've just got a few minutes, Miss Nellie. What can I do for you?"

"I wanted to tell you about the dead guy."

"What about him? Did you know him?"

"I talked to him," Nellie said with a vigorous nod. "He was outside last night, and I took his picture. He's been out there before. Sometimes he's talking on his phone. I have lots of pictures of him."

"When did you see him today?"

"He was out there before supper," Nellie said. "Tommy and I went to supper at Miss Jo's. He was talking on his phone, so I didn't bother him. He was yelling at someone, but sometimes he's laughing. He talks on his phone a lot."

"Was he there when you came back from supper?" Cora pulled a chair out and put her teacup on the table before sitting down.

"Yeah, but he was dead. I went over to ask him if he was all right and he didn't say anything, so I knocked on the door for Miss Gretchen."

"Did you see anyone else with him or talking to him? Or just anybody at all in the alley tonight?" Conrad furrowed his brow in frustration.

"I saw motorcycles tonight," Nellie said excitedly, and Conrad frowned at Cora. "I saw a lady with a purple ponytail with him once. I saw Mr. Levi outside there,"

Nellie said pointing to the other side of the building. "I saw Mr. Carey behind the spice store and a man with glasses at Miss Jo's."

"Where did you see the motorcycles, Miss Nellie?"

"They were driving down the alley when we were walking to supper."

"How many were there?" Conrad asked as he stirred creamer into the coffee that Cora handed him.

"Four," Nellie said holding up four fingers. "One motorcycle was really long and had a flag on it. One man had a yellow star on his back. They were really loud."

"Thank you, Miss Nellie," Conrad said standing up from the table.

"But Chief, I wanted to tell you I took pictures. I can get you pictures of all these people."

"Where's your camera?" Cora asked.

"Oh, Tommy carried it home for me, but I can make pictures of all these people for you. Wouldn't that help you?"

Conrad glanced sheepishly at Cora. "It might."

"Tommy will make those pictures for you, Chief, as quick as he can."

"Thank you, Miss Nellie. Now let me get you a ride home. I don't want you walking in the dark."

Nellie began to object, and Cora held up her hand. "I need a ride, too, so you can just come with me."

Sheri Richey

Chapter 4

After Cora and Nellie left in a police car, Conrad went back into the alley. Deputy Coroner Alan York was barking orders to two young men that had accompanied him.

"Put that marker there." Alan pointed to a spot near Booze Lockhart's foot and then waved the man out of the way while the second young man took a photo.

"Do you need anything, Alan?" Conrad had known the deputy coroner only a couple of years but knew he owned the largest funeral home in Paxton. Although he was efficient and knowledgeable, he did not have a soothing personality and had not been a good fit for greeting mourners. His funeral home had grown successful because he delegated the management of it from afar.

"No. We're about done here. Have you gotten all the photos you need? They're on their way to pick up the body now."

"I've finished," Conrad said leaning against his car. "Do you have any ideas about this one, Alan? I mean, cause of death? Did you find any marks on him when you rolled him?"

"Not a one," Alan said throwing up his hands. "I'll take a closer look when he gets to the morgue. Do you know anything about this guy?"

"Not much yet, but I'll get you a full profile tomorrow. I know he lived right outside of Red River, so he's a local. He has a wife in town. They're separated, but I'll need to contact her once he's moved. Hopefully, she can fill me in."

"Ask her about his health problems, who his doctor was and if he took any medication. Those things can help me. I'm going to run a tox screen. I smell alcohol on him."

"Yeah, I noticed that, too." Conrad pushed away from his vehicle when he saw an ambulance approach slowly down the alley. Alan waved them over as Conrad felt his phone vibrate with a text message from his dispatcher, Sam Crawford. Walking around to the back of his car, he tapped the phone number in the text message to call Kathy Lockhart.

Conrad listened to the phone ring until a voice message option was offered. "Mrs. Lockhart, this is Spicetown Police Chief Conrad Harris. It's very important that I speak with you at your earliest convenience. I will try back in about fifteen minutes and I hope we can speak then. Thank you."

Once Alan, his assistants, and the ambulance carrying Booze Lockhart pulled out of the alley, Conrad searched the area again. Booze had fallen into a bed of herbs that were planted neatly from the backdoor steps to the side of the inn. The plants were flattened to the ground by the weight of the body and Conrad sifted his fingers through the soil. A large indentation in the ground about three feet from the building and almost a foot deep was jagged as if something had hit that spot harder than the rest. The triangular indentation had been hidden by the body and lay under the center of where Booze was found.

Conrad knocked at the back door and Levi Nauchtman opened the door. "Come in, Chief. Is he gone?" Levi stretched his head out the door and looked around the alley.

"Yes, he's been taken to the morgue." Conrad walked up the concrete steps. "I hope we didn't disturb any of your guests."

"Not a one as far as I know. Booze was the only smoker and that's about the only reason anybody comes out back. Come in and let me get you some coffee."

Conrad sat at the kitchen table while Levi poured them both a cup of coffee. "Gretchen has gone up to bed. She has to get up really early to cook for everyone, so I cover the evenings and she does the early morning."

"I'll stop by tomorrow and chat with her," Conrad said as he stirred sugar and creamer into his cup. "Gretchen already told me about Nellie Turner finding him. What do you know about him?"

"A lot of bluster," Levi said shaking his head. "He thought quite a lot of himself. Talked all the time. I don't know if any of his stories were true, but he said he owned an interest in several businesses in Paxton and wanted to invest in Spicetown, too."

"Did he say what kind of businesses?"

"He mentioned a car wash and a gym in Paxton, but he talked like he owned a bunch of places. He was kind of a braggart."

"I saw him earlier today in the spice shop and there was a woman with him, a tall girl with blond hair that had purple painted on the ends. Was she staying here, too?"

"No, but she came in and out all the time. I think she lives nearby, but he called her his girlfriend, even though she was probably half his age." Levi sneered and shook his head in disapproval. "I think her name is Linda, but Gretchen might know more."

"I saw him take the key outside earlier. Did he always stop and get the key first before going outside?"

"Yes, the door automatically locks behind you when you go out the back."

"Had he been out there the whole time I was at dinner or did he come in and out while I was gone?" Conrad remembered Gretchen handing him a key attached to a long wooden handle with Nutmeg Inn carved into it.

"I didn't see him come in or out after you left, but I thought I heard him come inside when I was in the kitchen. Gretchen was at the front desk more during the evening than I was. She may have seen him."

"Does he have a car here?"

"No, he didn't ask for a parking place. I guess the girl brought him. We have very limited parking and we assign spots on the side when guests need a place."

"Can I take a look at his room?"

"Sure, Chief. Let me get a key."

Conrad took pictures of Booze's second floor room at the inn and was surprised with the disarray of his belongings around the writing desk against the wall. A plastic cup had spilled a brown liquid over the desktop and the saturated napkins were almost dry. There were loose coins and a small keyring on the floor around the desk, along with a receipt for dinner the previous evening, but no wallet. Deputy Coroner York had checked Booze's pockets before leaving and they were empty, except for a small disposable lighter. No keys, no wallet, no cigarettes, and no back-door key to the inn.

In stark contrast, the adjacent bathroom was spotless with each of his personal toiletries lined up precisely across the countertop like miniature soldiers. Booze had checked in the day before, but other than the desk, things were very neatly arranged. His shaving kit was carefully organized, and his towels still folded. Standing next to his toothbrush was a brown pill bottle without a label. After tossing the small yellow pills around in his gloved palm, Conrad let the pills spill out on the bathroom countertop and counted them. The bottle contained thirty-six pills with the letter "C" on one side and the number "50" stamped on the other side. Conrad put them back in the bottle before sealing it up in an evidence bag. The bottle would need to be fingerprinted.

A tall bottle of vodka and a small bottle of scotch were sitting on the bathroom counter with a drinking glass beside them. The vodka was still sealed but there was a fourth of the scotch missing. Conrad sniffed the glass before putting it in the evidence bag but did not detect any odor. The protective wrapping that the cleaning staff used to wrap the glasses was in the wastebasket along with a plastic purple flower.

After bagging all the individual items and labeling each one, Conrad looked through the small overnight bag again to open each zippered pocket. A second pill bottle labeled Fluoxetine was packed in the bag along with his neatly folded clothing for the next day. On the outside of the suitcase, a large zippered section held printed pages streaked with fading ink. They appeared to be printed Internet pages with an URL listed at the bottom of each page. The cover page was a search listing on his friend, City Attorney Ned Carey. Behind the search pages were printed articles focusing on a trial from 1981, long before Conrad had come to Spicetown.

The brown and green quilt covering the bed was wrinkled on the side closest to the window. A cell phone and TV remote control had both been tossed in the center of the bed. It appeared that Booze may have been watching television earlier, but it was not on when Conrad had entered the room. The cell phone required a pass code for viewing but Conrad had seen a charging cord in the overnight bag.

Conrad studied the windows of the room. The window by the bed was directly above where his body was found, and it was unlocked but closed. Conrad dusted the area for fingerprints even though he expected it would not be useful. The prints would be a collection of many prior visitors and cleaning personnel. The screen over the window was also intact with a sliding storm window raised to the top position of the metal track. It was clear that the window had not been his exit. Booze Lockhart must have walked outside to die.

Sheri Richey

Chapter 5

"Mayor," Amanda said jumping up from her seat when Cora appeared in her door.

"Morning, Mandy. Right through here, boys." Cora threw open her office door and pointed the two young men carrying boxes to enter. "Put them on the conference table for me, please. Oh... Good morning Larry. I didn't know you were in here."

"Sorry, Mayor. I was going to tell you..." Amanda walked around her desk.

"That's okay. I'll be with you in a minute, Larry," Cora wrinkled her nose and spoke quietly to Amanda. "Let me take care of him and then we'll lay out the route. Everything is all mapped out and looking good. Did you hear back on the color guard?"

"Yes. They've found someone and we have a couple of new riders, too. I've completed all their paperwork."

"Great," Cora said to Amanda and stepped aside to let the young men through the door. "Thank you for helping me get my boxes from the car. I appreciate it."

"Anytime, Mayor. Glad to help."

"Larry," Cora said walking into her office and leaving her office door open. "What can I do for you today?"

"I left messages yesterday and I didn't hear back from you." Councilman Larry Langley sat squarely in the middle chair across from Cora's desk.

"I got your messages, Larry. I'm sure you realize that it's a very busy time for me right now. I was planning to call you today." Cora opened the bottom drawer of her desk and dropped her purse inside before pulling out her chair to sit down.

"The parade is tomorrow, Cora. I have plans to make also."

"No, I don't really think you do," Cora said as she sat down and propped her elbows on her desk. "You will not be speaking at the dedication of the statue and I am not going to be able to include your daughter in my parade vehicle. There isn't room."

"Isn't room?" Larry stood abruptly. "There are four seats in that open car. Who is riding with you and the Spicers?"

"The Spicers brought their grandson with them and he is most eager to be involved. I met them last night and they are a delightful family. They will be riding with me." Cora rested her chin on her folded hands.

"I'm entitled to be a part of this presentation. I'm the senior councilman. I should be on that stage representing the town council at the dedication. It wouldn't look right. If you can't seat us all, at least I need to be present." Larry's face flushed, but he returned to his chair.

"Larry, you have done everything in your power to prevent me from honoring our town founder. You have fought this event every step of the way and been a leader in the opposition. This accomplishment does not belong to you. The townspeople will know why you are not on that stage."

"I'll not be slandered over your wasteful project. This statue doesn't fulfill any of the needs of the people of Spicetown. It was your selfish goal and I could not find any reason to support using town funds for frivolous decoration."

"Yes, I've heard this speech before and that's exactly why you will not be involved in the presentation." Cora stood from her chair and walked toward her office door. "I assure you, I will make it very clear to everyone present that the council was not responsible in any fashion. Only those who participated in a positive manner will be on stage with me when I speak."

Larry stared at Cora indignantly and seemed to search for words as he slowly stood.

"Now if you don't mind, Larry," Cora said as she grasped the doorknob of the open door and motioned him to exit. "I have a lot to do today."

"I'm going to speak with the council," Larry sneered as he walked through the door.

"You do that, Larry," Cora called out as he left Amanda's outer office area. Amanda winced once he had passed.

Cora Mae smiled mischievously and winked at Amanda. "Come on in, honey. Let's lay all this out on the table so we can see it. I needed a visual, so I mapped it all out in my living room floor last night. Come take a look and see if I missed anything. Once everyone starts to show up, it will be a madhouse out there and I need to be sure of everyone's placement."

Amanda smiled and followed Cora to the conference table. "Here, this box is where we start," Cora said as she pulled out a card to place on the table. "Conrad leads and then the fire truck. Here's the color guard." Cora turned her cards around to read from the side and lined them all up as Amanda studied them.

"I thought you wanted the scouts later, after the floats."

"I decided it was better to put them closer to the front so they could finish earlier. They aren't playing any music either, so the sound of the sirens won't interfere. I moved the bagpipers further back."

"So, they are coming?"

"Yes, I got an email yesterday that they will be here, and I want to make certain nothing interferes with their playing. They have a lovely sound. I moved the school band up in between the floats."

"Wow, this was a great idea," Amanda said gazing at the long trail of cards down the table. "You can really see it."

"It helps me," Cora said shrugging. "Sometimes my lists are just not enough. I've got cards for Market Day, too. That way we can get a bird's-eye view of all the vendors at the fair and make sure we've got them in the right position."

"Did you give me a good spot?" Amanda laughed. Bryan was setting up a booth at the Market Day Fair to show off his nursery plants and Amanda's decorative pots.

"They're all good spots!"

"I don't know how you do all this," Amanda sighed heavily. "You have worked such long hours on this. This is a lot."

"I love a parade," Cora said with a twinkle in her eye. "This isn't work. This is the fun stuff. Now, dealing with the City Council, I *have* to get paid for, but this, I would do this for free."

"It was pretty tense in here this morning with Councilman Langley," Amanda said grimacing.

"I always try to be diplomatic when dealing with the councilmen, but with Larry I've always had to be very direct. He pretends he doesn't hear things he doesn't like, so I have to be firm. It's the only way to shut him down. Dealing with the Council is not much different from being an elementary school teacher in a lot of ways." Cora smirked and rolled her eyes

"I don't think I could do that. He's very intimidating. I'm not good at that sort of thing."

"It's essential to be able to tell people what you want when it is important to you, Amanda. You should practice on Bryan." Cora giggled as Amanda blushed. "I practiced on Bing for years."

§

"Mrs. Lockhart?" Conrad removed his hat when a petite blond woman answered his knock on the door of a small single-wide trailer on the south side of Spicetown.

"Yes?"

"I'm Police Chief Harris. I wonder if I could speak with you for a moment?"

"Certainly. How can I help you?" Kathy Lockhart propped her elbow against the partially open screen door but did not move aside to invite Conrad in.

"I left you a few voice mail messages last night, when I wasn't able to reach you by phone. It's about your husband."

"I don't have anything to say about Booze," Kathy said snidely. "If you're going to serve me, just hand it over. We don't need to talk about it."

"No ma'am, I'm not here to serve court papers. Could we talk privately for a minute?"

"Mom. Who's at the door?" Kathy's head snapped back abruptly when the young female voice called out.

"My daughter is here." Kathy looked over her shoulder again and back at Conrad. "Just a second. Isabel, I need to step outside for a minute. I'll be right back."

Kathy stepped out on the top step to pull her door shut and Conrad backed up into the yard so she could step down. "Okay. What about Booze?"

"I'm sorry to have to tell you this, ma'am, but your husband was found dead last night."

Kathy stared off to the side for a moment and then met Conrad's eyes. "Did somebody kill him?"

"We haven't determined a cause of death yet. The coroner—"

"Somebody probably killed him, or his reckless lifestyle did him in. Where was he? Out at the Wasabi?"

"No, ma'am. He was found outside the Nutmeg Inn in Spicetown. I'm sorry I don't have any more details for you yet, but—"

"I don't need any. He's gone and the world will be a better place for it." Kathy heaved a deep breath and glanced back at her front door.

"I do have some questions I could use your help with, if you don't mind." Conrad pulled out his notebook and pen from his front pocket.

"Sure, I guess."

"Can you tell me who his treating physician is or anything about his current health?"

"He always went to Dr. Mason in Red River, but I know he's been going over to Paxton to some specialist. Dr. Mason might know."

"Do you know what he was being treated for?"

"No, we haven't lived together for almost two years, so I don't know what's going on with him now. I know he's gained a lot of weight this last year, but I don't know why."

"When you were together, did he take any medication?"

"Not that I knew about, but that doesn't mean he didn't. You might find out more from his girlfriend. I heard she was living with him."

"Did he abuse drugs or alcohol?"

"Boy, did he!" Kathy said with raised eyebrows. "Anytime he got a chance. That's why I didn't want Isabel around him. He told the judge last time we were in court that he'd given all that up, but I don't believe it."

"What exactly did he do for a living?"

"He invested in different businesses. He said he loaned them money to help them out and he got part ownership. He had his hands in lots of things and I really don't know what all he owns. That's part of what has delayed our divorce. The judge wanted a financial accounting of his assets and he kept dodging it. I know he's got money, but it's buried all over the place in different investments. He kept telling the judge he had no liquid cash and couldn't pay child support."

"Well, ma'am, I'm sorry about this, but you are his next of kin so the coroner's office will be contacting you."

"For what?"

"For funeral arrangements, once they are done with their assessment. They will need to know where—"

"I'm not burying him," Kathy said as she turned to walk away. "As far as I'm concerned, he can rot."

"Uh, one more thing, ma'am," Conrad said, and Kathy paused. "Where were you last evening?"

Kathy spun around with an angry glare. "Oh, you think I killed him? I was home all evening with my daughter."

"But I called, and no one answered."

"I don't answer the phone when I don't recognize the number. We were watching a movie and I didn't listen to the voice mail. I know everybody always wants to blame the spouse, but he wasn't worth the effort. There were plenty of people mad at him and I knew somebody would eventually end his life. I just had to wait it out and I'm not sorry he's gone. Maybe my life can have some peace now."

Conrad nodded sadly and let Kathy walk away as the phone in his pocket rang.

§

"Are you guys back here playing a game?" Conrad walked through Amanda's deserted office to find Cora Mae and Amanda moving cards around on the conference table and giggling.

"Yes, we are," Cora said smiling. "It's called follow the leader. See we have your card already played." Cora pointed to the far end of the table where an index card with a big star on it was at the head of the line.

"We are mapping the parade procession," Amanda explained with a shrug.

"The Cora Mae way, right?" Conrad laughed.

"Oh, hush," Cora said waving her hand at Conrad's teasing. "What brings you by for a visit? I thought you'd be all tangled up with work today."

"I just got a disturbing phone call while I was driving, and I thought it was just quicker to stop in here on my way back to the office."

"A disturbing phone call? About what?" Cora sat down at the conference table as Amanda quietly slipped out the door to go back to her office.

"The City Council has pulled the funding for my rent-a-cops." Conrad threw out his hands in defeat. "How am I supposed to manage the town's parade, fair, and fireworks without some extra manpower?"

"Oh, dear," Cora muttered and squinted her eyes.

"What did you do?" Conrad dropped into a chair across the table from Cora. "You did something, didn't you? And they're taking it out on me."

"No, now I didn't do anything, however I did—"

"So sorry to interrupt, Mayor," Amanda said standing in the doorway. "Laura just gave me this and it looks important." Amanda walked over and handed the paper to Cora. "She said Councilman Little brought it to her window and asked her to give it to you."

"Gordon Little is doing Larry's dirty work now, I see," Cora said lifting her reading glasses from their chain to read. "Well, it says they had a special meeting this morning to amend appropriations to allow for future expenditures to be met. There's no telling what all they've cut, but they know it will take time for me to fight this and we don't have time for that now."

"So, back to what you were saying." Conrad leaned forward on his elbows. "What happened this morning?"

"Well, it's all right. I expected this to happen. It's just earlier than I thought. I figured they would be angry after the holiday." Cora folded the letter back up and tossed it on the table. "It gives me something new to add to my statue dedication speech. I was just going to tell everyone how unsupportive they were regarding the statue, but now I can include their dirty back-stabbing tricks in there, too. They may feel pretty good now, but they forget how much I talk!"

"Cora, what's going on?"

"Larry didn't get his way this morning and now he's behaving like a child. Not to worry."

"Not worry! I need officers for these events."

"Keep your shirt on," Cora said scoffing. "How many do you need?"

"At least eight. Twelve would be better."

"Consider it done. You don't need police trained folks, right? You just need dependable reporters and conscientious people."

"Yeah, I guess. We can handle the calls, but we need bodies, a presence."

"Don't worry about a thing, Conrad. I can fix this. You'll have people. I promise."

Conrad gave her a wary glare.

"What's happening with the Booze situation?"

"Nothing much yet. I talked to his wife and I'm headed back to the office to call the Red River Chief to see if he knew him."

"Dan? I'm sure he did. He knows everybody around there. What was the wife like? Did she take it okay?"

"She seemed pleased," Conrad hunched his shoulders apologetically. "They've been apart a long time though and are going through a rough divorce."

"Don't forget Ned Carey," Cora said shaking a finger at Conrad. "You must have missed your coffee group today. I have to call him anyway because of this messy council business. I'll see what I can find out and let you know."

"Okay," Conrad said standing and pushing in his chair. "I'll let you get back to your card game."

"Don't make fun of me. I might just move your card behind the horses," Cora said cackling at her own joke as Conrad made a laughing retreat.

"Amanda," Cora yelled out the door to bring Amanda back into the room. "Run up to the council room and look in that storage closet up there. See if you can find those armbands we used during the 10k run last year and then bring in your notebook. We need to draft an ad to get in the newspaper today."

"Okay. Be right back."

Chapter 6

Conrad sauntered into the side door of the police department with a weariness that only too much to do can cause. He was going to have to make a Cora Mae list to sort it all out.

"Chief," Officer Roy Asher called out down the hallway before the door had completely closed. "There's a lady here to see you."

Conrad frowned and Roy advanced further down the hallway to meet Conrad at his office door. "Who is it?" Conrad picked up his water pitcher and walked to the break room with Roy on his heels.

"I don't know, Chief," Roy whispered. "Never seen her before but she's asking about the dead guy."

"She didn't give you her name?"

"Well, no, but she has purple hair."

"Oh, that must be Linda. Give me a minute to get the coffee started and send her back."

"Okay, Chief." Officer Asher spun on his heel to head out the door.

"And Roy," Conrad said. "Please remember to ask people their name next time."

"Yeah, yeah. Right." Conrad chuckled and shook his head as Roy hurried from the room.

Conrad poured water in his coffeemaker and waited for the trickling sound to begin before sitting down at his desk. He picked up a message slip that had been left there earlier saying Miriam Landry called and demands a return call. Crumpling it into a ball, he threw it into his trash can before turning on his computer.

"Chief?" Conrad looked up and Georgia Marks was at his door with his visitor. "Miss Lavender would like to speak with you."

"Thanks, Georgia. Have a seat. How can I help you?"

"My name is Linda Lavender. I saw you the other day in the spice shop."

"Yes, I remember."

"Well, I just went by the Nutmeg Inn to get Booze and the people that run it told me he was dead."

"Yes, ma'am, that's correct. How do you know Mr. Lockhart?"

"I'm his girlfriend. We met at the Wasabi where I work. I'm a dancer." Linda twirled the end of her purple ponytail around her finger. "Booze is an owner out there."

"He is? I wasn't aware of that. So, how long have you known him?"

"Since March," Linda said squirming in her seat. "What happened to him? Did he get sick? I don't understand how he could just die." Conrad noted some anxiety, but Linda didn't display any sadness.

"We don't know those details yet. Was March when he bought the Wasabi?"

"Yeah, he's a part owner. Wesley Parker still runs the place."

"Has he had any health problems you know about? Did he take any medications?"

"Yeah, he did, but I don't know much about that. You'd have to ask his friend, Stan. He took care of all that."

"His friend, Stan?" Conrad asked with raised eyebrows.

"Where is Booze now?"

"He's at the county morgue. His wife hasn't made the final arrangements yet." Conrad watched Linda closely for her reaction.

"Booze is divorced," Linda said with confidence.

"You know this?" Conrad said shuffling some papers on his desk.

"Oh, it just happened a few days ago," Linda said with wide eyes. "We were celebrating because Booze asked me to marry him. Did you talk to her? She knows."

"I'll check on it. Who is this friend, Stan?"

"Stan Tuttle. He and Booze have been friends since they were little. Stan has an office over in Paxton."

"What kind of office? What business is he in?"

"He does books. He keeps Booze's books, I know. Takes care of his money, you know." Linda stared out the window searching for words. "They do business stuff together."

"What business was Booze in?"

"He owned places. Lot of places over in Paxton. I think his family had money or something."

"Do you live in Paxton?"

"No, I live here in Spicetown. Well, really just outside of town in a trailer near the Wasabi. I was supposed to move to Red River with Booze this weekend. He wanted to wait until the divorce was final and all."

"Okay," Conrad said as he jotted her information down and got her phone number. "Does Booze have any problems with anybody? Any enemies?"

"You think somebody killed him?"

"We don't know why he died. I'm just covering all the bases."

"Booze didn't have any enemies, except maybe his ex-wife. Everybody loves Booze. He's a great guy and very generous. The girls at the club always love it when he comes in. He's been very good to me."

"The other day in the spice shop when Booze fell, you said you didn't know what had gotten into him lately. Has he had other falls? What made you say that?"

"He's not felt well lately. Really forgetful and he did fall one other time for no reason. He had a bug or something and said he needed some rest. Nothing big."

"Did he drive here? Is his car somewhere around the inn?"

"No, he asked me to drive. I usually do all the driving when we're together."

"Okay, Miss Lavender. Thank you for coming by and I'll contact you if I have any more questions."

Linda stood up and stopped at the door squinting her eyes. "Do you know if Booze had a will?"

"No, ma'am, I don't know."

"Do you know how I go about finding out?"

"I don't," Conrad said standing. "You might contact his attorney if you know who that is. They usually keep those things."

"I'll ask Stan. He'll know."

"Okay." Conrad smiled. "You have a good day."

§

"Good morning, Ned," Cora chirped when Ned Carey answered her call. "Did you expect my phone call? Do you know about the Council's shenanigans?"

Ned laughed heartily. "Good morning, Cora Mae. Indeed, I did, but it's always a pleasure to hear from you."

"My understanding of things, in a third-party backhanded way, is that the Council has pulled the money for the extra security this week during our 4th of July celebration. They didn't have the nerve to tell me to my face. Is that all they're up to?"

"That's all I know about."

"Well, that's no bother. I can take care of that myself. I just wanted to make certain they weren't tampering with other things that would ruin the event."

"As far as I know, that was the only result of this morning's meeting. Do you want to call a meeting on it to rebut?" Ned Carey was the legal counsel for the city and had helped Cora navigate these petty problems before.

"Not this time," Cora smirked. "I have other ways to resolve this. I just didn't want any more surprises when we are just a couple of days away from the parade. Let them have their fun."

"You're scaring me, Cora."

"There are always consequences when actions are taken for evil intent." Cora felt up to the challenge.

"If it's any consolation, I did advise them against doing this. One of these days maybe the Council will learn that underhanded tricks don't get them anywhere."

"I wish I still had that hope but dealing with them is too much like managing a bunch of fifth graders," Cora huffed as Ned laughed in agreement. "When you will risk the security of the citizens you should be protecting, just to get revenge for petty disagreements with me, that is something voters need to know about."

"I assume you plan to tell them?"

"Absolutely," Cora said with a smile in her voice. "There is one more thing I wanted to ask you about. Do you know Booze Lockhart? I saw him yesterday in your store and Karen said she thought you knew him."

"We've met," Ned said. "I heard that he died last night."

"Oh, you've talked to Conrad today?"

"No, just the morning coffee gossip. I guess the papers haven't gotten the story yet, but you know the rumor mill."

"Yes, I shouldn't be surprised. So, how did you meet him?"

"I met him the first time over in Paxton. I took my bike to Sharpe Auto & Motorcycle Repair to get some work done. He's the owner or part-owner of the place."

"You have a motorcycle? I didn't know that." Cora smiled at the mental image it created. Ned did not look like the type to be a motorcycle rider to her. He was well over sixty years old and not much taller than five feet. As he had aged, his waistline had grown to be almost as wide as he was tall.

"I do. I don't get out on it much anymore."

"So, he's a friend? Karen said he had asked for you when he was in the store in the past. Do you two ride together?"

"Oh, no," Ned scoffed. "He's just an acquaintance. He made an offer to buy the Sweet & Sour Spice Shop, but I turned him down."

"He was having some difficulty the other day. Karen said he just fell over and I was concerned he had some medical problems."

"Karen told me he damaged some stock and I told her to bill him for it. As far as I know, he was healthy. He's pretty pushy though. He just kept trying to contact me even though I told him I wasn't interested in selling."

"He did seem to have an assertive personality," Cora said. "I don't think Karen was fond of him either."

"He likes to get his way. He actually tried to coerce me into letting him at least buy into the store. I don't know why he wanted it so bad, but he got threatening at one point and that's when I stopped taking his calls."

"Threatening?" Cora shrieked.

"Yeah, he insinuated that he knew something damaging about me he was going to share. Something that would harm me professionally. I don't have any idea what he was talking about."

"Sounds like a bully!"

"Yes, he was." Ned agreed. "Maybe that whole act of falling over and damaging the store was some kind of payback. I was a little worried he would try to do some harm."

"Really? Good grief. I'll let Conrad know. It's possible his death wasn't accidental. With that kind of behavior, he could have a lot of enemies."

"That's true. He hung around a rough crowd. Although the mechanics at the motorcycle shop did a good job on my repairs, they were a scary looking bunch. Not a group you'd want to anger," Ned chuckled and coughed. "Called themselves the Buckeyes and had a motorcycle club they rode with. I don't know if Booze actually rode a bike though."

"Conrad may need to talk with you more," Cora said penciling herself some notes. "He's working on finding out more about Booze Lockhart. I don't think he even has a cause of death yet. He'll probably be in touch."

"Okay, Cora. You have a good day and don't let the Council get the best of you."

"Oh, I can handle them," Cora said with a chuckle. "But can they handle *me*?"

§

Amanda heard Cora's laughter from her office when she returned with the arm bands and peeked in the door to see if the mayor had a visitor. Cora motioned her into the room as she hung up the phone.

"Did you find them, dear?" Amanda walked into Cora's office with a tote bag in her hands and lifted one up to show Cora. "Yes. Yes, that's it. Now, let me see. I think you can remove those numbers easily and we can put some letters on there. What do you think? S-P-D and then A-U-X?"

"I'm sorry," Amanda said shaking her head. "What are we using these for?"

"The volunteers," Cora threw her hands up in the air. "For Conrad's security detail."

"Oh, I see."

"We can mark them as Spicetown Police Department Auxiliary and then everyone will be able to find them if they need them. It's not a uniform, but if we publicize it enough, everyone will know."

Amanda nodded and began pulling them from the bag.

"Now I just need you to take all the numbers off and replace them SPD AUX. Then put one on your arm and have Rodney take a picture of it." Cora patted her upper arm to show Amanda where they should be placed. "Did you bring a notepad? We need to draft a public notice for the newspaper and include the picture. We are going to ask the town for volunteers and explain to everyone what the bands mean."

"Okay." Amanda sat in a chair at the conference table. "You want the headline to ask if anyone wants to volunteer?"

"Don't ask. Tell." Cora waved a fist in the air. "Security Volunteers Needed for 4th of July Event!"

Amanda laughed at Cora's dramatic announcement.

"Now, tell them in there that we need volunteers for various details throughout the holiday event. Conrad will want people on parade duty, the Market Day craft fair and at night for the fireworks. Volunteers have to be over 18 and can sign up for just a morning, afternoon, or evening shift. I don't want anyone to miss out on events they want to attend."

"How do they sign up?"

"Why, they call you," Cora said laughing. "Put your name and your number here at City Hall. Make sure you get a phone number for everybody because Conrad will need to set up some kind of orientation meeting to tell them what to do. Tell Jimmy Kole to let all his staff know about this, too. Any of his staff of city street workers that are off work that day would be excellent choices."

"I'll work something up for you to look at," Amanda said as she turned to grab the box of arm bands.

"Oh, and make it clear there is no pay for this. It's just volunteering but it is a patriotic duty to show your love for Spicetown!"

"Got it," Amanda said with a nod of her head and a giggle.

Chapter 7

"Chief Fairmont."

"Dan, how are you? It's Conrad Harris over in Spicetown."

"Connie! It's been a month of Sundays since I've heard from you," Dan Fairmont laughed. "I bet I know what got you to call today."

"I have a situation over here involving one of your citizens. You've heard about it?"

"I sure have. Nothing official, of course, but I heard tell old Booze Lockhart turned up dead last night. My wife told me this morning."

"Yes, it won't make the paper until later today, but that never seems to slow down the news around these parts." Conrad always marveled at how fast news traveled in a small town.

"Well, her niece is friendly with Booze's wife, Kathy, and so my wife's sister called her this morning. We've known Booze since he was a boy. Went to school with him although he was a year ahead of me. Didn't get any details though. How did he die?"

"He was staying at the Nutmeg Inn and he was found dead behind the building. We don't have a cause of death yet."

"He wasn't shot or stabbed? Hmm…"

"No, did he have any health problems you knew about?"

"Aside from alcohol, drugs and women?" Dan laughed. "I wouldn't call Booze a health nut. I don't know about any specific malady though. I saw him about two weeks ago in Eddie's garage here in Red River. I guess he was getting his car looked at. He'd put on a bunch of weight and I thought maybe this bad divorce was slowing him down. I knew he and Kathy were separated but he doesn't spend a lot of time in town here."

"He was still living there though?"

"Oh, yeah. He lived out at Red River Ranch. It was his daddy's place, always lived there as far as I knew."

"That's why I'm calling," Conrad said shifting in his chair. "I need to get inside and look around a bit. Does anyone else live there?"

"Nope, not as far as I know. You want me to meet you out there?"

"Yes, if you would. I can't get over there until later this afternoon. I need to run to Paxton first."

"Checking on his businesses?" Dan asked. "He always said he had a lot of them over there. I know he had some interest in a gym in Paxton because I used to tease him about buying it so he didn't have to work out." Dan chuckled. "He was always kind of vague about that stuff."

"Do you know a Stanley Tuttle? I was told he was a boyhood friend to Booze."

"It's Stanford and yes, I knew him. He's a bit of a weasel, just like his daddy. I guess Booze knew him from Red River, but Stan is younger than us. I don't think Booze hooked up with him until later."

"Does Stanford live in Red River?"

"He's an accountant over in Paxton now. His parents are both dead and his brother moved away. His daddy was a wheeler-dealer like Booze. I never knew what he did, just dabbled in things here and there. Considered himself an entrepreneur. I never would have thought Stanford Junior would hook up with Booze though. Stan always seemed like a stuffed shirt. You know, too good for us small-town folk."

"So, where did Booze's money come from? Do you know?"

"I can't say for sure he even had any, but he always acted like he did. Beau Lockhart, Booze's daddy, owned a lot of property in these parts. Once Beau died, Booze sold everything except for the ranch and said he invested the money. Never said much else."

"Okay," Conrad said with a heavy sigh. "I'll give you a call when I'm headed your way and meet you at his ranch if you're going to be free later today."

"Unless I'm hit with a big crime wave," Dan said with a sputtering laugh, "I'll be here."

"Thank you, Dan. See you soon."

§

"Hey, Connie. I know you're busy, but I'm headed downtown to pick up lunch. I just called to see if you wanted me to drop something by for you?"

"Thanks, Cora, but I was just headed out of town. I'll have to grab something to eat in the car. I've got to run to Paxton."

"Okay, I just thought I'd ask. Oh, and I wanted to tell you I talked to Ned Carey this morning and I think you probably will want to do that, too."

"I didn't get to coffee this morning. What did he say? He knew Booze?"

"Yes. Booze was trying to buy the spice shop from him or invest in it. He didn't handle it well when Ned declined either. Seems Booze is a bit of a bully."

"Hmm, I'll give Ned a call from the car and see if he knows any of Booze's friends."

"He told me he met him at Sharpe's Auto & Motorcycle Repair in Paxton. Apparently, Booze owns that place."

"Explains why he might have known the guys at the spice shop that day. I'll check that out while I'm over there."

"Did you know Ned rode a motorcycle?" Cora still hadn't come to terms with that knowledge. "I just can't see that. Can you imagine Ned flying down the road on a bike?"

"Seems like he mentioned it once. I don't think he rides much anymore."

"Ned said the motorcycle club that hangs out there is called the Buckeyes. If you get to meet them, invite them to the parade. I think they'd make a nice addition," Cora said giggling at the scowl she envisioned stretching across Conrad's forehead.

"I think I'll leave the parade promotion to you," Conrad laughed.

§

"Tabor," Conrad said as he walked out to dispatch.

"Yeah, Chief?"

"I need you to check on something for me. Booze and Kathy Lockhart were in divorce proceedings and I need to know where that stands. Miss Lavender was in here earlier and she says it was finalized, but Mrs. Lockhart led me to believe it was still pending. I need to know the truth."

"Sure thing, Chief."

"Oh, and ask them for the name of Booze's legal firm. I may need to call the attorney later."

Officer Tabor nodded vigorously and walked over to an available desk.

"Georgie?" Conrad said as the dispatcher, Georgia Marks, ended a call. "I'm headed over to Paxton if you need me. Call ahead and let the Paxton PD know I'm coming, will ya?"

"Okay. Paulie Childers from the Spicetown Star has called for you a couple of times. He needs to talk to you to confirm some details before his deadline."

"I'll give him a call," Conrad nodded to Georgia. "Hey Asher, what time does the Wasabi open?"

"Uh," Officer Asher blushed as everyone looked at him with a grin. "I don't know, Chief. I think around four o'clock or so."

"I'm headed to Red River after I leave Paxton, so I may not be back in the office before shift change. Call me if you need anything."

§

"Mayor?" Amanda carried her box of arm bands back into Cora's office and dropped the box in a chair across from Cora's desk. "Here is a draft for the paper."

"Thank you," Cora said stretching out her hand for the paper. "Conrad told me those Buckeyes are in Paxton at the Sharpe Auto & Motorcycle Repair Shop. Can you call and invite them to the parade?"

"Sure."

"Oh, and are the arm bands ready?"

"Yes, that's the other thing. I wanted you to look at these—"

"Oh Mandy, those look fabulous!" Cora stood from her desk and reached out to take a closer look. "That's as nifty as a pocket on a shirt! You did a great job."

"Thank you." Amanda's cheeks colored from the praise. "You didn't mention what color so I—"

"They're perfect. They look very official."

Amanda spun around when she heard a soft rap on the mayor's door. "Excuse me. Mayor?"

"Come on in, Jimmy. Amanda was just showing me the arm bands for the volunteers. She told you about that?"

"Yes." Jimmy Kole walked in and picked up an arm band. "They look really nice."

"I think so, too." Cora handed the arm band back to Amanda. "How can I help you?"

"Well," Jimmy said, "that's actually why I stopped by. I sent the word out to my guys about the volunteer effort and I've got six interested. Some are working at putting out the trash receptacles and picking up the bins so they can't help, but the ones with the day off were on board. Rodney is busy doing your filming of the parade and dedication during the day, but he said he'd volunteer for the fireworks detail."

"Wonderful news," Cora said throwing her hands up. "Amanda will need their names and phone numbers. Conrad will have to brief them at some point."

"Rodney is off work tomorrow and asked if you had plans for the Spicer family. He was going to offer them a tour of town if you needed that."

"That sounds splendid! I don't know if they have any plans. They might just be planning to shop, but I'll leave a message at the Nutmeg Inn for them and let them know that Rodney will call to check with them."

"Okay, I'll tell him to contact them there with his offer."

"Let me get those names and numbers of your volunteers down," Amanda said running back to her office as Jimmy followed.

"You need to run this article over to the Spicetown Star before two o'clock," Cora hollered.

"Okay," Amanda yelled back. Conrad was going to have so much help they might all be falling over each other out there on the 4th of July.

§

"Thanks for calling back, Chief. I need to get this to print today," Paulie Childers said over the Bluetooth speaker in Conrad's car. "We don't get a murder in Spicetown every day."

"Murder?" Conrad shouted. "Paulie, you can't print that. We don't have anything to suggest it was a murder."

"Well, what was it then? You don't just die in the alley for no reason."

"We don't know the cause of death yet. It just happened last night. The coroner is working on it."

"Well, what details can you give me?"

"Paulie, I'm driving. I don't have anything to give you. I thought you wanted confirmation on what you had. Read it to me."

"Oh, well, it's not all written yet, Chief. I have Beauregard Lockhart of Red River Ranch, age 58, was found dead in the alley behind the Nutmeg Inn on Ginger Street at approximately 8:00pm on Monday, July 1st."

Conrad blew out his breath. "I think you could soften that statement a little bit, but it's not incorrect."

"Yeah, yeah, I'm working on it, Chief. That's just the rough draft. Who found the body?"

"I don't think that needs to be in the paper."

"Well, everybody says it was crazy Nellie Turner, but I also heard that Levi Nauchtman called it in."

"You heard that, did you?" Conrad crinkled his nose in a sneer. "I can't confirm either of those statements. What else do you have?"

"Just that Lockhart was a co-owner of the Wasabi Women dance club out on Clover Road. I hear he owned some businesses in Paxton, too."

"I can't confirm any of that yet either."

"How about a statement? Can you give me a quote?"

"The cause of death is undetermined. The county coroner's office is investigating. How's that?"

"Okay, I guess," Paulie said with a disappointed pout to his voice.

"Just remember when you're writing this that this man has a wife and teenage daughter living in Spicetown. Try to be sensitive to that."

"Sure, Chief. Will you let me know when you find out more?"

"I can't promise that. Good talking to you, Paulie. I've got to go." Conrad hit the dashboard button to disconnect the call and shook his head.

After a few more bites of the sandwich he had picked up to eat on the drive, Conrad tapped his dashboard phone again and let it dial Ned Carey's number. He needed to get the details on the information Cora had shared with him.

"Hey, Ned. How's it going?"

"Hey Connie. Cora said you'd probably call. Missed you at breakfast."

"Yeah, well, it's been a busy day. I just wanted to see what you know about Booze Lockhart. Do you know who he does business with or what all he owns?"

"I can relay what he told me, but I don't know if it's true. He was a bit of a blowhard, so I was skeptical."

"I hear he bought into the Wasabi, but I haven't talked to Wesley yet to confirm that. Did he mention any other businesses in Spicetown?"

"No, just Paxton. He said he owned a gym over there and had office spaces he rented out somewhere near Industrial Park."

"I'm headed to Paxton now. I'm told he had an accountant over there doing his books. Have you ever heard of Stanford Tuttle?"

"Sure. I've met him a few times. He handles a number of business accounts. I had a lawsuit over there with Barnaby Metals and he did the payroll accounts for them. He did a good job, but he's an odd little guy."

"How so?"

"Just kind of quirky, fidgety, you know. I don't think he's comfortable around many people. He was sweating on the witness stand and nervous as a cat."

"Was he being accused of anything? What was the case about?"

"No, he was just testifying about the billing. His work wasn't being questioned. Barnaby Metals buys scrap metal and they cheated a bunch of people when they weighed the metal. They didn't pay them what they should have. Tuttle was just recording what they received. His part wasn't in question at all."

"Did you win?" Conrad chuckled.

"Of course, I did," Ned replied with a hearty laugh. "I try not to take cases I can't win."

"So, Cora said Lockhart tried to coerce you into letting him buy into the spice shop?"

"Yeah, he first wanted to buy it. When I told him it wasn't for sale, he started offering me investment money. He wanted to be a partner and said we could expand. Once I turned that down, he upped the ante and started getting really pushy. I had to stop that."

"What was he doing? Just wouldn't give up?"

"Started really trying to threaten and intimidate me. I have to admit, it worried me some. He acts a little crazy when he gets upset. He said he had some dirt on me and could ruin my career. Never told me what it was though. He's the kind of guy that's used to getting his way. He can't take no for an answer. I started avoiding all contact with him and haven't heard from him in about a month."

"That may be why he was in the spice shop. Maybe he was looking for you."

"Karen told me about the mess he made. She doesn't like him very much, anyway."

"Cora and I were just outside the store when we heard the crash."

"Yeah, we lost a lot of products. Karen had just made up a big batch of pumpkin spice. She mixes it herself and he took out the table where she had been working so we lost it all."

"Karen is the one that told me she thought you might be a friend to Booze, since Booze asked her about you during earlier visits."

"I never told Karen that Booze wanted to buy the place, but when she called about the spill the other day, I told her if he asked about me again, she could tell him I moved to Nebraska," Ned laughed. "I let her know he wasn't a friend and he wasn't anyone I wanted to see."

"Ned, did Booze ever mention any legal work to you? You know, ask you about any of your cases in the past?"

"Not specifically, but he kept implying that he knew all about my legal career, made comments about skeletons in my closet and things like that. One day when he called me and got angry on the phone, he said that he knew I was a crook and he would let everyone else know, too. That's when I told him to go pound salt and hung up on him. I've not talked to him since that day."

"No idea what he was talking about?" Conrad wasn't ready to ask Ned about the trial in 1981 yet. He preferred to know all the answers before he asked questions.

"No idea, but I'm not a crook, Conrad."

"And I'm not implying you are, Ned." Conrad chuckled to relieve the tension he sensed from Ned's tone. "I just thought he might have given you some hints as to what he was poking around at."

"No, just idle threats."

"Cora said you met him at a motorcycle shop in Paxton. If I have time, I might try to stop by there and see what they can tell me. Is it on the west side of town?"

"Yeah, it's on the edge of town just past the flea market. It's called Sharpe Auto & Motorcycle Repair."

"I'll swing by if I have time. Thanks, Ned."

Chapter 8

Conrad's first stop in Paxton was the county morgue. Opening his trunk, he pulled out the sealed evidence bags containing the medication he found in Booze's room at the inn. The rest of the evidence was already locked up at the police department and Conrad had emailed his report to the coroner's office. He didn't know what the unmarked pills contained, so he needed to drop them off for analysis.

Conrad was not familiar with the young girl at the counter and she seemed uninterested in helping him as he approached.

"Hello, I'm Conrad Harris from Spicetown. I just needed to drop off some evidence for the Booze Lockhart death last night. I emailed—"

"Here, fill out this form," the young woman said as she pushed a paper across the counter toward Conrad without making any eye contact.

"Okay," Conrad said slowly. "Do you have a pen?"

The woman looked around and then smacked a pen firmly down next to the form.

"Thank you," Conrad said warily. "Is the coroner in? Or Deputy Coroner York?"

"They're not available right now." The young woman sat down at a desk several feet behind the counter and turned to her computer.

Conrad began filling out the form and pulled his cell phone from his pocket. The young woman was not paying him any attention, so he scrolled through his saved numbers and tapped the name Alice Warner. Turning to the side, he put the phone to his ear.

"Alice? This is Conrad. I'm out front with those medications."

"Well, come on back Connie. I've got a few preliminary results from the first toxicology screen I can show you. We had to send some of them off to the lab, so they aren't back yet. Angie should be out there. Just tell her I said—"

"That's okay. I just wanted someone to know I was dropping these off. You can email me the results of the tests if you're busy."

"Oh, are you in a big hurry?"

"Well, the young lady up front said you were not available." At those words, the woman's head swiveled sharply, and she peered angrily at Conrad.

"Pfft," Alice huffed. "Hang on."

The door to the back of the room swung open and Coroner Alice Warner filled the opening with a scowl on her face. "Angie, let Chief Harris in, please."

The woman stood slowly and opened the door on the side of the reception counter for Conrad to step inside.

"Come on back, Connie," Alice said as she pushed the door shut firmly behind her. "I tell you, that girl…"

"She's not terribly inviting," Conrad said.

"That's why we never put her out front, but Cindy is off this week, so we're shorthanded." Conrad followed Alice down the hallway and into her office. "I guess you won't be surprised that we found alcohol in his system."

"No, not at all. We could smell it at the scene." Conrad took a chair across from Alice's desk.

"That's what Alan said, but he was surprised when we saw the results were at a very low level. He wasn't intoxicated at all."

"Maybe he spilled it on his clothing," Conrad said. "I found alcohol in his room at the inn and the dried remains of what looked like a liquid spill."

"Probably, but we'll test the clothing." Alice pulled a page out of her folder and held it up to reference. "He had drugs in his system, not your typical recreational sort, but anti-psychotic. I'm going to see if they match with what you brought in today. The levels were really high, unusually high. Did this guy have a mental disorder?"

"Not that anyone has told me about, but I haven't talked to the doctor listed on the pills yet. One bottle is prescription and the other is unmarked."

"We sent a request to them for medical records after we got your report this morning. The fluoxetine he had the prescription for is an anti-depressant, but the doctor writing the script isn't a psychiatrist. He's a general practitioner, a family doctor."

"So, you think maybe an accidental overdose?" Conrad couldn't see someone taking excess medication and then going outside. *Why wouldn't Booze stay in his room if he planned his death?*

"Could be or it may be a suicide. I can't even say for sure it is the cause of death until we are done with the physical exam. I just thought you could use a heads-up. I'll send over the medical records when we get them, but I think we're going to find more in his system than one isolated drug. His screening came back with some really unusual results. It could be he was experimenting with various cocktails. Was he a recreational drug user?"

"There's been some mention of drug use, but I don't have any specific information yet. I was curious about the unmarked bottle. They might be street drugs."

"I should have that information for you by this evening."

"Great. Thanks, Alice. Talk to you soon."

Conrad went a little out of his way when he left the coroner's office. He wanted to drive by Sharpe's Auto & Motorcycle Repair Shop and take a look at it before he went to Stanford Tuttle's office.

Winding around the road near the flea market, several motorcycles passed him, and he noticed that none of the drivers wore a helmet. It wasn't legally required in Ohio, but he thought it was the wise thing to do. Driving slowly by, he saw a large sign that said Sharpe Auto Repair. There were open garage doors and several cars in the parking lot.

After he passed by and turned around at the next street, he saw the motorcycle entrance. It was on the side of the building and it was one large open end with dozens of bikes parked outside. The sign above the entrance read Motorcycle Shop and he could see people sitting inside. There were some bikes being repaired, but it looked more like a club meeting than a business. A large white sign with the picture of an Ohio buckeye hung on the side of the entrance without any caption. He knew his visit was not going to be a welcome one.

Stanford Tuttle's office was at the end of a long row of small connected businesses next to tool rental center in the industrial part of town. It seemed out of place when the rest of the businesses were small niche retail shops rather than offices. It was not where he would expect an accountant to be located, far from the financial district of Paxton.

All the parking was available, and Conrad parked squarely across from the entrance. After he updated dispatch to his location, Conrad got out of the car and walked to the glass door. He noticed there were no lights on inside but saw a small reception desk that was neat and tidy. Pulling on the door handle, he found it locked.

There were hours on the door and a phone number so Conrad returned to his car and called the number. After leaving his contact information on Tuttle's office voice mail, he called the station.

"Georgie, is Tabor in the office?"

"Hey, Chief. No, he's out on a call. Do you need him?"

"Check with him and see if he has a home address for Stanford Tuttle."

"Okay. Hang on." Conrad could hear Georgia Marks contact Officer Tabor over the radio as he waited. He hadn't wanted to give Tuttle a warning, so he hadn't tried to call him before leaving Spicetown. He had wanted to get a fresh impression of Tuttle and talk to him before he prepared his thoughts on Lockhart. Cora Mae would call it an ambush, but he preferred to see it as unrehearsed. He had hoped Tuttle would prove to be a close contact to Lockhart, someone who truly knew his daily movements, since no one else had provided any deep insight.

Linda Lavender had indicated Tuttle was a friend who took care of Booze's needs, and only someone close would know about his health and medication. Surely, Booze had a real friend somewhere.

"Sorry, Chief," Georgia said returning to the phone. "Tabor said all he found was the address on his driver's license, but that was in Red River. It's probably old. Nobody would live in Red River and drive all the way to Paxton to work."

"Text it to me, anyway. I'm headed to Red River next and I'll check on it. It may have been his parents' place. I think he grew up in Red River."

"Okay, Chief. Will do."

"One more thing. When Tabor gets back in the office, have him see what he can find out about a motorcycle club in Paxton called the Buckeyes."

"Gotcha," Georgia said quickly before switching over to answer a radio call.

"Thanks." Conrad disconnected the call.

Georgia was probably right. Red River was west of Spicetown and Paxton was east. It would be more than an hour of driving each way to work and that didn't seem likely. He suspected Tuttle still had his family home and just kept using that address. Then again, he might be driving right through Spicetown every day.

Sheri Richey

Chapter 9

Conrad left Paxton without visiting the motorcycle shop. He wanted to talk to Tuttle before he met up with Sharpe. With the looks of the place, he might need to take another officer with him. There was strength in numbers and despite Cora Mae's teasing, his experiences with motorcycle clubs had not been positive.

About ten miles out of Paxton, his phone rang, and he tapped the blue tooth receiver.

"Harris."

"Hello, Connie. I can tell by the echo you must be in the car," Cora Mae said. "I won't keep you. I'm just calling to see if you want to go out to eat tonight. I'm leaving the office shortly."

"Well, I'm headed to Spicetown now, but I've got to go out to Red River so I'm just passing through."

"Oh, are you going to see Dan?"

"He's going to meet me at Booze's ranch so we can look around. You can ride along if you like. We can eat over at Flo's Diner in Red River after. I haven't been there in ages."

"Sounds like the best of both worlds," Cora said. "You can get me caught up on the investigation during the drive. All the gossip coming in and out of city hall today was enough to choke a horse."

Conrad laughed. "I'll be in town in about thirty minutes. Will you be home by then?"

"I should be unless something unexpected blows in my door."

"I'll pick you up at home then."

"Okay, see you soon!"

§

Upon arriving at Red River Ranch, Conrad's spirits had lifted. He had a lot weighing on his mind. Cora had done what she could to lighten his mood.

"See how much easier this would have been if you'd made a list? Now I know all the details, I can make one for you. You'll see. It helps straighten out your mind," Cora teased.

"My mind isn't crooked," Conrad said smiling.

"Like Ned?" they both said in unison and then roared with laughter at Conrad's retelling of his phone conversation with Ned Carey earlier that day.

"We should be about there. I think the house is up this way," Conrad said nodding his head.

"I see two cars," Cora said pointing. "Is somebody living in the house?"

"No, I don't think so." Conrad pulled in beside a small black car and then saw a white truck parked on the side of the house.

"Dan is over here," Cora waved to Dan Fairmont who was leaning against his police car.

"Let's go see what's up," Conrad said as he released his seatbelt and opened his door.

Dan began sauntering towards them working a toothpick in the side of his mouth.

"Hi there, Cora Mae. It's good to see you."

"And you," Cora replied. "How's the wife?"

"She's doing well. We've not been to Spicetown in a while though," Dan said tossing his toothpick onto the gravel driveway.

"Well, you need to get there on the 4th. We're having a big shin-dig, you know," Cora said patting Dan's arm. "Tell Evelyn I said hello."

"I sure will," Dan said and then looked sheepishly at Conrad as he walked around the car. "It seems we have a situation here."

"Is somebody living here?" Conrad frowned as he looked at the house.

Cora jumped when she heard barking and a large tri-colored Australian Shepherd ran towards them but stopped when Cora held out her hands to him. After a few cooing words, the dog came to Cora and enjoyed a rub behind the ears. "She's just a young pup," Cora said soothingly. "She's a beauty."

"It seems that the missus has moved back home," Dan said with raised eyebrows. "Sometime today she got some fellows to help her move her stuff in and she's nesting right here. Says it's her house now."

"Legally it may be," Conrad shrugged. "Assuming she's on the deed, but I still need to get in there and look around."

"She didn't seem interested in cooperating when I first got here. You can take a shot at her if you like. Maybe you'll have better luck."

Conrad nodded and walked slowly to the front door studying each step as he approached. He didn't have to knock on the door because Kathy opened it as he stepped on the porch.

"Mrs. Lockhart," Conrad said reaching up to tip the bill of his hat and then remembered he wasn't wearing one. "I called Chief Fairmont before I came by, because I'd like to look around the place, if I can. This is actually Chief Fairmont's jurisdiction, so if you'd rather he handled it—"

"No, I don't want him in here. I don't have to let him in here. This is my house now." Kathy Lockhart held the door open just wide enough to show her face. "Is that the mayor?"

"Yes, she came with me, because we have another errand after this visit."

"Well, you two can come in, but not Dan Fairmont. He's another of Booze's cronies. He let Booze get away with anything he wanted, because they were friends. He's not my friend."

"I'll talk to him," Conrad said and then tried to look around. "Is there anyone else here? Is your daughter home?"

"She's spending the night with a girlfriend in Spicetown. I have a friend here who helped me move my things in today."

"Are your husband's personal belongings still here? I just need to look through his things and see if it can tell me anything about his health or his business dealings. We still have a lot of questions to answer."

"I just moved in today. I'm unpacking now."

"Let me talk to Chief Fairmont and I'll be right back." Conrad turned to walk back to Cora and Dan just as he heard the door click shut.

"Well, she says she's okay with me going inside and I can bring Cora. She sees you as a buddy to Booze right now and doesn't want to let you in," Conrad said to Dan. "Are you okay with that?"

Dan looked down at his feet as he shuffled them in the dust. "Guess so," Dan said shrugging. "I don't know what she's got against me. I don't think we've even met before. I used to see Booze in town off and on, but she was never with him."

"Booze may have led her to believe he had the upper hand with you, because of your past and that's why she sees you as Booze's friend," Cora said trying to soften the situation.

"You know how domestics are," Conrad said referring to police calls answered when partners argued. "Booze may have threatened her with his local police connection."

"True. I can see him doing that, too." Dan smiled. "Go on in before she changes her mind. I'll stick around until you're done. Who's in there with her?"

"She said a friend helped her move today and the friend is still here. Her daughter isn't home though."

Conrad nodded at Cora and they headed for the house with Dan leaning back against his vehicle again.

§

"I told her we had another errand to run after this visit and that's why you were here," Conrad said just above a whisper. Cora nodded and followed him up the porch steps just as the door opened.

"Mrs. Lockhart, this is Mayor Bingham," Conrad said as Kathy Lockhart opened the door fully to allow them to enter. Conrad motioned for Cora to go first.

Cora shook Kathy's hand and smiled. "I don't believe we've ever met."

"No, but I know who you are," Kathy said as she closed the door and locked it behind them. "Please have a seat." There were boxes stacked along the open bar area of the kitchen and several against the wall, but the living room was tidy. "I know it's messy in here, but I've got to go back to the apartment tomorrow morning and get the rest of our stuff."

"No worries," Conrad said as his eyes scanned the room. "Did your husband have an office or a work area here?"

"Yeah, it's right over there through those French doors." Kathy pointed to the open doors off the side of the living room and sat down on the opposite end of the sectional sofa from Cora.

Conrad went into Booze's office and was not surprised that the desktop was neatly arranged just as the bathroom at the inn had been. He slipped on his latex gloves and took some pictures around the room while he listened to Cora Mae chat with Kathy Lockhart.

"Mrs. Lockhart, are you from Red River originally?"

"Oh no. I grew up north of here, in Athens, Ohio."

"I guess you moved here when you married?" Cora shifted in her seat when she heard a noise in the back of the house.

"No, not right away. Booze was living in Athens when I met him. He only wanted to move back here because of the house. When his dad died, he had to come back here and take care of things."

"I don't know many people from Red River. I don't think I ever met your father-in-law. I suppose your husband grew up here?"

"Yeah, but he left when he turned eighteen. His mom died when he was young, and he didn't get along with his dad at all."

"Oh, that's a shame."

"Yeah, I never even met him," Kathy said standing abruptly. "I'm sorry. I didn't even think to offer you anything. Would you like some water or...? I'd have to look and see what's here."

"Oh no, dear. I'm fine." Cora waited for Kathy to sit again. "Well, we're always sorry to lose a Spicetown resident, but this seems like a really nice place."

"Thank you. I always liked the house, but it is kind of out in the middle of nowhere. My daughter isn't too happy with the move."

"How old is she?"

"She'll be fourteen next month."

"Ah," Cora said smiling. "Friends are everything at that age. I'm sure she will be missing them."

"We've only been gone from Red River for two years. There are kids here that she knows, but starting

89

high school is traumatic." Kathy rolled her eyes and smiled. "Teenagers."

"Yes, but I'm sure once school starts and she sees some familiar faces, she'll settle right into this beautiful place."

"Ma'am," Conrad said from the office door. "I'd like to take this laptop with me if that would be okay."

"Uh, I don't know," Kathy said springing off the couch. "I will get it back, won't I?"

"Sure. Sure," Conrad soothed. "I'll have it back to you real soon and I'll give you a receipt and all for it."

"Okay," Kathy said settling down again on the sofa. "My daughter could really use that for school. She doesn't have one.".

"I'd like to check his bedroom if I could," Conrad said as he leaned over the sofa and put the laptop next to Cora. "And did he have a central place in the house where he would put his wallet or keys, empty his pockets when he came home?"

"On his dresser usually, back here," Kathy said springing up again and leading Conrad down the hallway.

Cora jumped and turned her head when she heard a knock at the door. The top of the door was beveled glass and she could make out the shape enough to know it was not Dan Fairmont.

"Mrs. Lockhart," Cora called out. "There's someone at your front door."

Kathy trotted down the hallway back to the living room and stopped abruptly with a wary expression. "I don't know who that is," Kathy said to Cora as she slowly turned the deadbolt lock and eased the door open a few inches.

"Hi, I'm Linda and I have some things I left here I'd—" Kathy slammed the door shut and threw the dead bolt lock. Cora jumped up.

"Chief," Kathy called out as she headed down the hallway. "I need you to tell this stripper to get off my property."

Returning with Conrad following, Cora sat back down, but turned sideways in her seat.

"I'll talk to her," Conrad said as he turned the bolt and stepped outside.

Conrad held his hand up to encourage Linda to back up away from the door. "Miss Lavender. I know—"

"Chief, my stuff is in there and I just want to pick it up. She's got no right to keep my stuff." Dan Fairmont walked slowly toward the porch.

"We can make arrangements to collect your things and get them to you, but right now is not the best time." Conrad looked over at Dan as he reached the steps.

"What do you have in there?" Dan said trying to draw Linda off the porch. "Come with me and let me make a list. We can get it for you."

"She shouldn't even be in there," Linda pleaded. "That's not her house."

Linda reluctantly followed Chief Fairmont back to his car and Conrad tapped on the door he had heard Kathy Lockhart bolt behind him when he'd walked out.

"Everything's okay."

"I want her out of here, Chief. She's got no right coming here."

"I take it you know Miss Lavender?" Conrad said as Kathy threw the deadbolt again.

"I know who she is. Some floozy Booze picked up in a strip club."

"She has left some of her personal items here and she'd like to get them. Chief Fairmont is making a list with her and I'll get them to her. You don't have to bothered with it."

"Personal items," Kathy huffed. "I want them all out of here."

"I'll just be a few more minutes," Conrad said as he walked back down the hallway to Booze's bedroom.

"Okay," Kathy said as she blew air up through wispy bangs and flopped back down on the sofa. "I'm sorry, Mayor. I just don't need that right now."

"I understand perfectly," Cora said. "These things can get touchy and a death always heightens emotions."

"Oh, I'm not sorry he's dead. In fact, that's the only break I've caught in the last two years," Kathy chuckled nervously. "I'll have to thank the person who did it, once Chief Harris catches them."

Cora frowned. "But your daughter, she's lost a father."

"No, he was never a father to her. I don't think he knew how to be." Kathy shrugged her shoulders and lean sideways to curl her feet up on the sofa. "She's better off."

"Do you plan to stay here?" Cora asked. "I mean, you're happy living here?"

"For a while," Kathy said wistfully looking off toward the corner of the room. "I don't have anywhere else to be right now, but once Isabel gets out of high school, I'll probably sell and move then."

"Well, you're welcome to come back to Spicetown," Cora said cheerily. "You should really try to come to town for the 4th of July. We have a wonderful day planned. There's a parade and the Market Day Craft Fair during the afternoon. Then there is a firework display at dusk. I'm sure Isabel would enjoy it."

"I'll probably be working on moving in still," Kathy smiled politely.

Conrad came back down the hallway. "Okay, ma'am. I think I'm about done here for now. I just need to run out to my car for a minute and get my receipt book for the laptop and then we'll be on our way."

"Okay," Kathy said following Conrad to the door to let him out.

Conrad had a receipt book in the zippered case he had carried into Kathy's house along with evidence bags and labels, but he needed to get the status on Linda without bringing up her name.

"Do we have everything worked out here?" Conrad approached Dan and Linda as they stood using the trunk of his car as a desktop.

"I think so," Dan said ripping a piece of notebook paper from his pad and handing it to Conrad. Taking a quick look to make sure he understood the items, he nodded and headed back to the porch.

Seeing Kathy's profile through the glass top of the door, Conrad pivoted and went to his car to pretend that he was getting something out. Keeping the peace sometimes meant he had to take a few extra steps.

When he reached the porch, Kathy opened the door for him. "Is she leaving now?"

"As soon as I collect her things," Conrad said holding the paper out for Kathy to review.

Pushing it back at him, she turned and sat down again. "I don't want to handle her things. Can you please do it for me?"

"I'll be right back." Conrad glanced wearily at Cora and headed down the hallway.

Opening the lower cabinets in the bathroom, Conrad pulled out various female personal items that seemed to match the list and tossed them into a large evidence bag. There were make-up items, hair products and an assortment of purple plastic flowers similar to the one he had found in the wastebasket in Booze's room at the inn. There were only a few items of female clothing hanging in the closet and he grabbed those to cover all his bases. As he lifted the hangers from the rod, he saw a small wood paneled door in the back of the closet with a porcelain knob. Pulling the door open, he saw a thick stack of paperwork neatly piled in the cavity and tossed the bag of Linda's items on the bed. Reaching inside to remove the papers, he saw plastic bags behind them and pulled that out also.

Bagging all of those items and softly closing the door, he zipped them in his carrying case, wrote out an evidence receipt for Kathy and walked back to the living room.

"Would you like to take a look, ma'am? There are a few clothing items here and I don't want to take anything that might be yours."

"Nothing of mine has been in Booze's bedroom for years, Chief. Anything you want in there you can have."

"Alrighty then," Conrad said taking a deep breath. "We'll be on our way now. If I need to come back for any reason, I'll be sure and give you a call before I come, now that I know you're living here."

"Okay, Chief. That's fine," Kathy said standing and following them both to the door. "Please don't forget the laptop. Isabel needs that before school starts."

"I should have it back by then. I won't forget. Thank you for your cooperation today and if you think of anything... Oh, there was one thing I wanted to ask," Conrad said stopping abruptly before reaching for the door. "Do you know a Stanford Tuttle?"

"Ugh, yes. Stan is, was, Booze's business partner. They owned some things together."

"You aren't fond of him?" Conrad was puzzled by Kathy's look of disgust.

"No, he's creepy. I never have liked him, but Booze thought he was an easy take."

"An easy take?" Conrad asked quizzically.

"Booze likes to do business with people who don't ask many questions. He had some shady dealings and he didn't want anyone prying into his business. Stan wanted to give him money to invest for him and pretty much did whatever he told him to, so he liked him. At least he liked doing business with him. I don't know that he actually liked him."

"I see. Well, I haven't talked to him yet, so this is helpful. Thank you."

"Sure," Kathy said as she glanced outside first before opening the door wide for Conrad and Cora to step out.

"Have a nice day," Conrad said again reaching for the cap that wasn't there. *Where was that hat?*

Linda Lavender met them as they walked toward the cars and followed them back to where Dan was standing while she looked through the bag.

"All there?" Conrad asked with a hopeful look at Dan Fairmont. Waiting for her reply he glanced over at the vehicle she arrived in and tapped the license plate number into his notepad on his phone. He didn't think a dancer at the Wasabi could afford a luxury car and he wanted to check for the registered owner. No car for Booze Lockhart had been located yet.

"Yes, I think so," Linda said slowly. "Those clothes aren't mine though." Linda crinkled her nose in a sneer.

"Okay, I'll take these. Miss Lavender, do you know how to reach Stan Tuttle? I tried his office today, but he wasn't there."

"Yeah, he lives here in Red River," Linda said pointing down the road. "Just on the edge of town there."

"Yeah, just a lick down the road," Dan said nodding. "I can get you an address." Conrad thanked him as they parted company, but he thought he probably already had that address.

Once Conrad reached his car, he saw a man lifting a box from the back of the white pickup truck parked on the side of the house. He had shoulder-length black hair and a white shirt on with Sharpe's Auto & Motorcycle Repair scripted across the back in red lettering. The man glanced over his shoulder and quickly carried the box around the back of the house before Conrad could call out to him. He did notice that Linda smiled and waved at the man as she opened her car door to leave.

§

"Well, that was entertaining," Cora said with a satisfied grin as soon as Conrad started the car. "Did you find anything?"

"It was much as I expected," Conrad said. "His belongings were neat as a pin, just like the room at the inn. He's a fastidious man so that spill on the desk was either caused by a struggle he had with someone or he fell down like he did in the spice shop. But, if he fell, I would expect him to clean it up right away. That seems like the type of thing he would do, unless he couldn't for some reason."

"He spilled his drink and knocked things off the desk," Cora said thinking aloud. "Then he walks downstairs and goes outside without the back-door key?"

"I called Gretchen this morning. She told me that Booze took the key from her when we were there in the lobby with the Spicers and he never gave it back. She didn't hear him come back inside."

"But you said Levi told you he thought he heard him return," Cora said pointing her finger.

"Yes, but he's not sure."

"Maybe it was the killer that Levi heard coming inside. Maybe he knocked Booze out, took the key, came inside looking for something and made the mess."

"Killer?" Conrad chuckled. "I don't think we're there just yet and the coroner's office hasn't mentioned any contusions. It's leaning toward an overdose, accidental or not."

"Sometimes people that exhibit a lot of confidence are really insecure. His bragging may have just been overcompensation for how he really felt about himself. Kathy said he had a bad relationship with his father and his mother died when he was young."

"You're a psychologist now?" Conrad laughed when Cora scowled at him.

"I'm exploring all options," Cora said with her chin in the air.

"You may not be far off," Conrad admitted as he turned into the parking lot of Flo's Diner. "Alice Warner told me that the prescription he had was an anti-depressant. I still don't know what the other drug was, but I'm hoping I hear soon. Could be just because of the divorce though." Conrad parked the car and they walked to the front door. Pulling the diner door open for Cora, they saw a sign to seat themselves and Conrad followed Cora to a table.

"Are you getting the medical records?" Cora asked pulling menus out from behind the napkin dispenser and handing one to Conrad.

"Alice has already ordered them."

"Well, that should tell you whether it's situational depression or a lifelong problem."

"Alice said he had high levels of an anti-psychotic in his bloodstream, not an anti-depressant. Maybe he did have mental health issues he didn't share with other people. If it's regulated right, there's no need to."

"Maybe, but Kathy should have known. They were married for a long time I assume. I mean their daughter is fourteen."

"You don't have to be married to have a child," Conrad laughed.

"I know that," Cora scoffed. "So, what do you think about this Tuttle guy?"

"I don't know if he's avoiding me intentionally or just unaware I need to talk to him. I tried to surprise him by just dropping by his office today."

"You don't want to be the canary in the mine," Cora said nodding agreement.

"Exactly. When he wasn't there, I left a voice mail on his office number. Maybe he hasn't heard it yet. Pretty strange that he lives in Red River and works in Paxton, though. I wouldn't want to drive seventy miles to work every day."

"Maybe he doesn't go into the office unless he has an appointment. He could have a secretary that handles the office and he works at home. He's from Red River. That's home to him. What are you going to do with the laptop?"

"It needs a four-digit code to open it. I didn't expect Kathy would know what it was since they've been apart a few years. She doesn't really seem to know much. If I can't figure it out, I'll have to send it to the state lab."

"Did you hear her say she's from Athens and she met Booze there? I wonder what he was doing up there, besides avoiding his father. What did his father do? Do you know?"

"Dan Fairmont said that his father owned a lot of property and that Booze sold it off once his dad died. He also told me that Stanford Tuttle didn't live in Red River when I asked him."

"Do you think he doesn't know Stanford is living here?" Cora thought policemen always stuck together, but this was not the first time she had wondered if that were true.

"Look at the size of this place," Conrad said waving a hand toward the front window at the main street of town. It was only about four blocks long and that was all there was to the downtown. "How could he not know? I just don't know why he would try to mislead me."

"Maybe Kathy was right. Maybe he was a close friend to Booze and is covering up something."

"He admitted to knowing and seeing Booze. He said they went to school together, but that Stanford was younger, and he acted surprised that Booze would befriend him."

"Very curious," Cora said as the waitress approached to take their order.

Chapter 10

"That was such a nice treat," Cora Mae said as she fastened her seat belt and Conrad slid into the driver's seat.

"It was, but I think I may have to move my car seat back because my belly is hitting the wheel." Cora giggled as Conrad reclined the seat slightly. "Nothing fancy, but just good home cooking."

"It always makes me ask myself why I don't cook more often. You know, I cooked dinner every night before Bing died."

"But you weren't Mayor of Spicetown back then. He was." George Bingham, Cora Mae's husband, had been mayor of Spicetown for years and everyone called him Bing. Cora had retired from teaching to take Bing's job after his passing.

"True, and it's not easy to cook for one person. It just doesn't seem to make sense," Cora said as Conrad backed the car out of the parking space.

"If you ever need a volunteer, I'm always available," Conrad said glancing at Cora before pulling the car out on the main street of Red River.

"I thought you didn't cook."

"I don't. I meant a volunteer eater. Then you can cook for two and I'll make sure there are no leftovers."

"Deal," Cora said laughing. "Once things settle down after the holiday events, maybe I'll do that."

"Now, you know there will just be something else. You'll get done with this parade and—. What's next? Back to school supply drives? Labor Day celebrations? Octoberfest? It's always something."

"It's important to keep the citizens engaged in their community," Cora said stabbing her index finger in the air indignantly.

"I'm not knocking it. I'm just saying—"

"I know. I know." Cora raised an eyebrow when Conrad turned down a shady residential street before driving out of Red River. "Are you going to check on Stanford Tuttle?"

"Yeah, I thought I'd drive by and see if it looks like he's living there. Tabor gave me an address earlier, but I just thought he hadn't updated his driver's license. I didn't think he was still living in Red River."

"If he is, do you want to stop?"

"No. I'm going to give him tomorrow morning to contact me. That's long enough for a secretary or someone to get my voice message and pass it on. If I don't hear from him by lunch, I'm going to hunt him down."

"Surely he knows that Booze is dead by now. Anyone who hears a friend, or a close colleague has died, would naturally want to help the police."

"Anyone who is a law-abiding citizen," Conrad added with a smirk. "I'm not sure about this Tuttle guy though. Tabor pulled a bunch of research on him for me and he's got his hands in a lot of pots. Maybe it's just business but he has some questionable business associates. People tend to associate with people that share similar interests."

"Birds of a feather... Um," Cora said nodding in agreement.

"It should be just up here on the right at the end of the street," Conrad said pointing.

"There's a car here," Cora said grabbing for her purse. "Let me write down the plate."

"No need," Conrad said tapping his index finger against his temple. "I got it right here." Cora giggled as Conrad smiled. He always teased her about making lists of things and pretended not to need those, but this license plate number was already in the notes he'd gotten from Tabor. He recognized the vanity plates.

"It looks like a Halloween haunted house," Cora said frowning. "I'm glad it's not completely dark outside yet."

"It's in a bit of disrepair."

"Could be a sign of financial difficulties."

"It could also be he's not handy, or he's rarely home. Not everyone values the outside appearance. At least the yard is mowed." Conrad turned the corner to head back to the main highway.

"It doesn't look inviting. I wouldn't want to go knock on the door."

"From what I've gathered, he's not a terribly social guy. I think he's intelligent, but uncomfortable with interactions. Ned Carey told me he's met him. He had to testify in some trial and was quite anxious being on the witness stand, even though he wasn't in any trouble himself. I asked around about him to some Red River people I know, and they knew who he was, but little else."

"One of my clerks is from Red River. I'll ask her tomorrow and see if she knows anything about him."

Conrad glanced over when he heard Cora tapping away on her phone. "Are you making a note of that?"

"I am," Cora said huffily. "Laugh all you want, but I like order. My notes and my calendar give me order."

"I understand," Conrad said holding up his hand in defense. He made his own notes secretly, only because he liked teasing Cora about hers.

"I also have a note here reminding me to tell you about your security detail."

"I have a security detail again?"

"I told you I'd take care of it," Cora said fanning both her hands out. "They need to be briefed tomorrow though. Amanda will organize it for you. She'll call them all together so you can give them instructions. What time would be good? Could you be at City Hall at five o'clock?"

"I think I'll have Wink take care of it, but five o'clock is fine."

"I'll let her know." Cora began tapping into her phone to email Amanda that she would see when she arrived at work the next morning.

"I guess you have a busy day planned tomorrow?"

"Oh, yes. Just finalizing the route, making sure everyone knows where to be and when to be there, lots of ducks to get in a row, but all the big stuff is done. Amanda has been amazing. She's a whiz at all this stuff."

Cora took a deep breath. "You must be looking at a busy day tomorrow, too. I hope this little murder isn't going to take you away from my parade."

"Of course not," Conrad laughed. "I wouldn't miss it. I just need to make the most of tonight and tomorrow."

"Tonight? What are you doing tonight?"

"After I drop you off, I'm going by the Wasabi. I need to talk to Wesley, and I think he sleeps during the day."

"We will be driving right by there in a mile or two."

"Yes, I know, but I didn't figure you wanted to stop at the Wasabi," Conrad said smiling. "Wesley won't be happy to see me. He thinks I cramp the style around there when I walk in. The guys regularly buzz around the parking lot each evening though. We're trying to keep the place honest."

"I've driven by before and it looks a little intimidating to me, but I must admit I am a little curious. The dancing girls in there do have clothes on, right?"

"They do," Conrad laughed. "It may be the size of a quarter, but it's clothing. It's the touching law that gets tricky. The law doesn't allow the employees to touch the patrons. I know they do it and that's usually what we catch when we walk in unannounced."

"There it is," Cora said pointing. "A lot of motorcycles there."

"Yes, it draws a lot of bikers. The parking lot has as much trouble as the inside. We get called out here for fights from time to time."

"Well," Cora said with a heavy sigh, "I think I'll pass. I might upset the applecart and I certainly would feel uncomfortable."

"I don't think you'd enjoy it," Conrad said with a chuckle.

"Are you looking for the purple pony-tailed girlfriend? Or are you just wanting to talk to Wesley?"

"Linda Lavender still works there. I found out her name is really Linda Sneedman, but I need to talk to Wesley about his business deals with Booze."

"I'm surprised Wesley partnered up with anybody. He's had this place for a long time, and I thought the business was doing well."

"It's hard to tell. It's a popular place but he may be overextended. Some people don't manage money well," Conrad said as he reduced his speed to enter Spicetown. "I'm going to pull over here for a second." Conrad slowly coasted to a parking place on Fennel Street.

"Everything's closed," Cora said frowning.

"I know. I just want to let this car pass by." Conrad glanced in the rear-view mirror just as a black sedan passed by and then Conrad pulled back out behind it. "This car has followed us from Red River, and it looks just like Tuttle's car."

"Surely he couldn't have gotten out of his house to pursue us that quickly."

"Hmm, apparently so," Conrad said as he braked behind the sedan to allow it to turn. "Same plate, same car."

"Coincidence?"

"I think not." Conrad's brow wrinkled in thought. "I think someone's paranoid about unexpected company and wanted to know who we were or where we were going."

"Well, turn behind him," Cora shrieked and put her palm against the dash. "Let's follow him and see where he's going."

"Cora, he knows we're behind him."

"So what? It can't do any harm. Let's see what he does about it."

Conrad shook his head and slowly turned the car onto Paprika Parkway, keeping a safe distance from the sedan until it pulled into the parking lot of the Old Thyme Italian Restaurant.

Cora's head jerked quickly towards Conrad. "Where are you going? Why didn't you turn in?"

"We've already eaten," Conrad said smugly as Cora fumed.

"But he may just be turning there to get rid of us. We should have turned in."

"No. That would have just forced him to go inside. If he's avoiding us, he'll turn around and leave. That's why I'm going around the block."

"Oh, okay," Cora said leaning back against her seat with resolve.

Conrad drove down the block and turned into the alley that ran behind the restaurant.

"Look, there he is in the back," Cora pointed and scooted forward in her seat. "Who's he talking to?"

Conrad pulled his car in beside Joann Biglioni's car by the back door so they could watch Stanford Tuttle. Joann was the owner's daughter and ran the restaurant most of the time. Tuttle's car window was down, and he was talking to someone who was leaning toward his window.

"I can't see him," Cora whined. "We're not in a good spot."

"Just wait," Conrad said. "He's got to back out or the guy will walk off. Either way, we'll see them."

Cora hit the button to lower her passenger window to see if she could hear. There were muffled sounds of conversation, but nothing identifiable. Soon the sounds of crunching gravel were heard as the man walked away from Tuttle's car and toward the front of the parking lot.

"I'm pretty sure that's the same guy that was out at Booze's house today. He was driving the white truck parked on the side of the house."

"When did you see him? I didn't see anybody," Cora said.

"When we were getting in the car, he was beside the house. I guess he was out back when we were inside."

"So, which one should we follow?"

Conrad laughed at Cora's enthusiasm. "Neither one."

"Well, don't you want to know what he does next? Surely he didn't drive all this way for a conversation in a parking lot. He could have done that on the phone."

"Uh huh." Conrad could think of many reasons why there might be a conversation in a parking lot, but he chose to just hum in agreement with Cora. Conrad backed the car out of the parking space and drove down the alley, turning to circle back the way he came. Parking across the street from the Old Thyme Italian

Restaurant, he waited for movement. "Let's just see if he leaves and heads back towards Red River."

Several minutes passed and a white truck pulled out with Tuttle's car following. The truck turned right towards Paxton and Tuttle's sedan turned left towards Red River.

"Well, I guess they did just meet to talk." Conrad shrugged.

"That makes no sense," Cora hissed. "We need to find out who that other guy was."

"You can put that on the list for tomorrow."

Sheri Richey

Chapter 11

After dropping Cora off at home, Conrad headed back to the Wasabi Dance Club and pulled slowly into the parking lot. There were at least a dozen motorcycles parked together and another dozen cars sprinkled throughout the lot. Conrad drove his car around the side and towards the rear side entrance door because it opened by the bar. The front entrance opened to tables encircling a stage.

Walking in the door, he saw Holly Campbell wiping down the bar. "Hey, Chief. What can I get you?"

Holly never scowled at him as the other bartenders did, but she didn't greet him with a smile either. "I need to speak to Wesley."

"He's back in the office. Want me to get him?"

"No, that's fine. I'll go back there." Conrad was actually relieved to get away from the loud music and dim lights. The atmosphere was not meant for conversation.

Winding down the back hallway, he found Wesley Parker sitting at his desk in a tiny office only large enough for two.

"Chief," Wesley said jerking his head up in surprise. "What brings you by?"

"I just had a few questions. Do you have a minute?"

"Sure. Sure. Have a seat." Wesley waved his hand toward the only chair in the room. It was turned sideways with the back against the wall because there wasn't room for any other arrangement. "Questions about what?"

"I'm sure you heard Booze Lockhart is dead."

"Yeah, I heard."

"I understand you two were business partners."

"He was an investor," Wesley said leaning back in his chair to recline against the wall.

"So, what does his death mean to you? How does it affect the Wasabi?"

"I don't rightly know yet," Wesley said stretching in his chair until the springs squeaked. "I've got someone looking into that for me."

"You know he's married, right?"

"I've heard that, but he never mentioned it to me."

"You may have a new business partner," Conrad said raising an eyebrow in hopes Wesley would react. "Who handled the contract business for you? Do you have an attorney?"

"Nah, just a financial guy. He's gettin' it all together for me. We never directly discussed what would happen if he died, to tell you the truth. I mean, who does that? I never thought to ask."

"So, you don't know if you are now full owner or whether his wife is your partner? He could have even left his investments to someone else in a will."

"Does he have a will?" Wesley abruptly leaned forward, and the chair groaned.

"I don't know," Conrad said innocently. "People that are well-to-do tend to do that kind of thing."

"Yeah," Wesley said rubbing his chin and looking away.

"Did you get along well with Booze? Were you friends before he invested?"

"Nah," Wesley said shaking his head. "He came in here a few times and told me he really liked the place. Said we could franchise it and open one in Paxton. He's dating one of the girls here."

"Yes, Linda," Conrad said nodding. "Did this all happen last year?"

"It's not been quite a year, but—"

"And has he done anything about opening a new place in Paxton?" Conrad hadn't heard anything about these plans materializing.

"He's been looking for a good location," Wesley said. "Hadn't found the right space yet."

"Ah and has he actually given you money?"

"Well, no," Wesley said as his eyes darted over his desktop. "He was going to rent the new space in Paxton and get it started. It takes a lot to clean up the place, get it staged right, hire staff and girls. He was going to take care of all that."

"In the meantime, is he taking a cut of profits here?"

"Yeah, he gets a payment," Wesley shrugged. "Just a percentage to help him get the new place up and running. He's fronting all those costs in Paxton."

"But, as far as you know, there haven't been any costs yet. Is that right?"

Wesley just scrunched his shoulders up around his ears and held out his hands. "Maybe. I don't know."

"Wesley," Conrad said and waited for Wesley's full attention. "This doesn't sound like a profitable agreement for you. You were paying Booze and getting nothing for it."

"I thought it would be," Wesley pleaded. "I still think it could be. Paxton is a big place. There's a lot of potential."

Conrad raised one eyebrow and tilted his head back in a mocking glare. "I think you're smarter than that. Did he have something on you? Did he threaten you in any way?"

"What? No, Chief. Why would you think that? Some people didn't like him, but he made a lot of money with his business deals and I think he could have made me a lot of money, too."

"Come on, Wesley," Conrad said slapping his hand firmly down on the desk. "I've known you too long to buy this. Tell me the truth."

"Got nothin' to tell, Chief." Wesley dropped his chin and look up at Conrad innocently.

"Well, you must be special," Conrad sneered. "I hear he bullies people until they sign away part of their business and then Booze never puts out anything."

"Is that so?"

"It is," Conrad said standing up. "If your financial guy is any good, I think you'll find out that you've been taken, but good luck with that."

"Wait, Chief," Wesley shouted before Conrad's foot had crossed the threshold of the tiny office. "How'd he bully them into it? I mean, what'd he do?"

"You tell me," Conrad said with his hands on his waist.

§

"Morning, Mayor," Amanda chirped as Cora bustled in the door of Amanda's office with an armload of files and notebooks.

"Good morning, Amanda. We have only one day left. Are we ready?" Cora walked through Amanda's office into her own and dropped the stack of files on the conference table before going to her desk to stash her purse in her desk drawer.

"Yes, I think we're in good shape," Amanda said leaning against the door frame to Cora's office and holding up her notepad. "All the volunteers for security are gathering in the lobby of City Hall today at five o'clock for their briefing."

"Good," Cora said pulling out her chair to sit. "How many did we end up getting?"

"Twenty-seven."

"Oh my," Cora said giggling. "Conrad only asked for six."

"Actually, I turned some away." Amanda squinted her eyes with remorse. "I was concerned about some of the volunteers being… Well, maybe not a good fit for the assignment."

"I trust your judgment," Cora said waving her hand dismissively. "No explanation necessary. Sounds like we have plenty of civic-minded individuals to handle the task. I plan to heap praise on all of them in my dedication speech and shame the City Council for their underhanded move."

"I'll stay late tonight and manage the front door for the Chief since it's after hours."

"He said he was planning to send Wink instead. Conrad is really strapped for time right now with the incident at the Nutmeg Inn. Wink is switching shifts so he will be available during the day and can drive in the parade."

"Okay," Amanda said checking one item off her list. "The Spicers are meeting Rodney here at ten o'clock this morning for a town tour. He asked if he could give them a sneak peek at the statue. I told him I'd ask you if that was okay."

"Certainly! I don't know why I didn't think of that myself. We have drawings here also. Make them some copies to take home so they'll be able to share it with the rest of their family."

"Will do," Amanda said. "The schedule is on your desk and I've notified everyone in the parade of their placement and report times. Jimmy Kole has notified everyone signed up for Market Day. There's a map on your desk of the booths. His staff are going out to the park tonight and early tomorrow to help all the vendors set up."

"Will there be a podium and microphone set up by the statue?"

"Yes. Rodney is doing that in the morning so he can get the camera placement set ahead of time. How many chairs do you want up there?"

"Just four, I think. One for me and three for the Spicers. I'm not inviting any of the Council to participate, given their attitude, and Conrad is just too busy. I don't want to obligate him."

"I'll let Rodney know." Amanda tapped her notebook with her pen. "I think that's everything. Did we forget something?"

Cora rustled papers around her desk to check her lists and frowned. "No, I don't think so. This is going too smoothly. It's making me nervous."

Amanda laughed and then raised her eyebrows. "Oh, I forgot. Nellie Turner was here this morning when we opened. She was waiting at the front door. She said she has to talk to the Chief, and I guess she thought you could get that message to him. She acted like it was urgent."

Cora sighed. "I don't think Conrad has time for that right now and frankly, he's not likely to take the time for Nellie. I'll pass it on, but if she comes back by, try to get her to tell you what's going on. Maybe it's something I can take care of for him."

Amanda nodded and turned to go back to her desk, but then stopped. "You know, Mayor, people make fun of Nellie and her brother all the time because they walk around town. I know they're different, but Tommy is actually really smart. I don't know Nellie very well, but Tommy was in school with me. He's very quiet. He hardly ever says anything, but when he does, he's pretty amazing. He had good grades, and…"

"I understand. People make assumptions about their intellect because their behavior seems outside of the norm. I believe Tommy may be autistic and it doesn't mean he is intellectually impaired at all. I taught many children over the years with varying limitations. It's different for everyone. Tommy may be brilliant, but just have barriers with social interaction or practical skills. I didn't have him in my class, though, so I don't know for certain."

"People are cruel sometimes," Amanda said frowning.

"I prefer to think they're just uninformed." Cora smiled as Amanda shrugged and returned to her office.

Cora pushed the power button to start her computer. It was time to finish her speech for tomorrow.

§

"Are you awake?" Conrad chuckled when Officer Hobson answered the phone groggily. Switching from night shift to day shift abruptly was hard on everybody, but Wink had asked to be a part of the event this year.

"Yeah, I'm… Actually, I'm not sure. I'm trying to be," Wink said groaning. "Maybe this wasn't such a good idea after all."

"About the time you get accustomed to days, it'll be time to switch back."

"I know, but I'm awake now. What's the plan for today, Chief?"

"I told you we lost the security detail, but the mayor set us up with some volunteers. They need to be briefed on their duties and you'll need to figure out where to station them for the best coverage. They're meeting at City Hall this evening at five o'clock. I'll need you to handle that."

"Sure, no problem."

"If you're awake and ready to start the day, I'd like you to take a ride with me to Paxton. I've got a couple of places to visit and I could use the company."

"Are you interviewing?"

"If I can find the people I need. Have you ever heard of the motorcycle club called the Buckeyes?"

"Yeah, I've seen them cruising around town. I don't know much about them, though. They were involved in a little altercation out at the Wasabi a couple of months ago. I talked to one of them. I think his name was Montana, but nothing much came of it. We got a call of a fight, but when we showed up, they were just gathered in the parking lot and nobody was talkin'."

"Well, they hang out at a repair shop in Paxton and I'm hoping to talk with the owner there. Booze Lockhart had some investment in the business, and I think the bikers knew him."

"I'm up for it."

"I'm also trying to nail down his accountant. He has a business in Paxton, but it wasn't open when I checked on it. He lives over in Red River so I may have to go back there if he doesn't call me."

"Give me ten minutes." Wink sounded fully alert now.

"Okay. I'll fill you in on the drive over there." Conrad disconnected the call and glanced up as Georgia Marks appeared in his office doorway. "I'm going to pick up Wink and head back to Paxton."

"Before you go, Chief, Nellie Turner has been by the station early this morning. She said she needs to talk to you about some pictures. She said she took some pictures of some people in the alley the night Booze Lockhart died, and you wanted to see them."

"Did she leave the pictures?" Conrad's eyebrows shot up in surprise.

"Well, no," Georgia said shifting from one foot to the other. "She didn't give me anything. She said she needs to talk to you."

"I don't have time for this right now, Georgie. I don't think she has any film in her camera, if you get my meaning."

Georgia laughed and nodded. "I know, Chief, but she's very anxious."

"She always is." Conrad rolled his eyes. "If she comes back, you just tell her I'm away from town and she needs to leave them with you."

"I'll try," Georgia said as she spun on her toes to race back to her dispatch desk.

Glancing at the time, Conrad picked up the phone to return a call to Booze's divorce attorney. He had tried to reach them the day before and they had returned his call.

"Good morning. Attorney Vanderhaven's office. Can I help you?"

"Good morning. This is Chief Harris from the Spicetown Police Department. I'm returning a call to Scott Judson."

"Just a moment."

Conrad tapped the top of his pen on his notepad impatiently and glanced at the clock again while he listened to a local radio station play during the hold. A commercial was running for the Paxton Fitness Depot offering a reduced monthly rate for new customers and Conrad added a note to his list. Booze was involved in some personal gym in Paxton and that might need to be another stop for him.

"Good morning, Chief. This is Scott Judson. I got a message you called about Booze Lockhart. Terrible tragedy. How can I help you?"

"Well, I'm looking into his death and I'm getting some conflicting information about his marriage and financial status. I'd hoped it was something you could shed some light on."

"Something specific you were interested in?"

"My research suggests the divorce was not final, however, Mr. Lockhart had told several people that it was. Was something in the works when he died?"

"It was, yes. We had reason to believe the divorce would have been finalized by the next court date on July 8th. We were waiting for Mrs. Lockhart's attorney to confirm, but we felt an agreement had finally been reached that was satisfactory to both parties."

"I see," Conrad said clearing his throat and realizing he would have to rely on Kathy's attorney to supply those details as Mr. Judson was being vague. "An issue, as I understand it, throughout the proceedings centered on Mr. Lockhart's financial solvency and his various investments. Can you provide me with a list of the businesses he invested with or owned?"

"That's a very complicated issue, Chief. I don't have a simple list to give you. We have records from his accountant and tax information he provided. We've struggled to work through all those details to satisfy opposing counsel, but his investments were varied."

"So, no," Conrad said bluntly. "You are not providing me that information?"

"Well, Chief, of course I want to help…"

"Yes, I can hear that in your voice," Conrad said sarcastically. "If you prefer I use legal means to extract that data, I will do so."

"I'm not trying to be uncooperative."

Conrad rolled his eyes. Attorneys were always uncooperative and self-serving. "No, I get it. I just thought since the man is dead you would have an interest in the greater good. I am just trying to determine if there is any reason someone would try to do him intentional harm. His cause of death is still undetermined."

"Oh, I had heard it was a suicide."

"Rumors are not always reliable, Mr. Judson," Conrad said curtly. "You have a good day."

Not waiting for a reply, Conrad hung up the phone and grabbed his hat to go pick up Wink for the drive to Paxton.

"The Spicer family is here." With Amanda's announcement, Cora hit the save button on her speech draft and jumped out of her desk chair.

"Good morning!" Cora embraced Ellen Spicer and shook young Bradley's hand.

"Good morning, Mayor. We are here to meet a young man that works for you. He's offered to give us a tour." Mike Spicer put his arm around Ellen's shoulders.

"Oh, yes. Rodney Maddox. He works for our street department, but he has many other talents," Cora said wiggling her fingers in the air and smiling. "He thought you might enjoy a guided tour today and maybe a peek at the statue."

"Oh, cool," Bradley said excitedly. "Can we go to the popcorn factory, too?"

"Well, that factory actually closed many years ago and the city bought the building. We're getting ready to remodel it so it can be used for community events. Right now, I'm afraid it's just a big empty building, but you can certainly go by and look in the windows. It is an unusual place."

"Oh, I didn't know it was closed," Bradley said glumly. "I saw it when we drove in."

"When it was in operation, it made the town smell like a movie theater all day," Cora said laughing. "It was wonderful."

"I wanted to ask you," Mike Spicer said, glancing at Bradley with indecision, "about the status of the little incident from the other evening? Has anyone determined what happened?"

When Cora paused to structure her reply carefully, young Bradley Spicer jumped in to clarify. "He wants to know about the dead guy."

"Bradley," Mike scolded as Ellen put her hand on her chest and looked off in the corner of the room. "Don't be disrespectful."

"No, it's all right," Cora said smiling. Children could always be relied upon to say what everyone else was thinking. "Chief Harris is working on that."

"Is he going to do an autopsy?" Bradley's eyes were wide with excitement. "You know, he has to do that to find out what killed him."

Ellen reached out and placed her hands on Bradley's shoulders in an attempt to calm his momentum.

"Chief Harris doesn't do the autopsy, but—"

"Bradley, that's enough of that," Mike said sternly, and Bradley stepped back. Cora could see that the light had gone from the young man's eyes. Children's questions could seem inappropriate at times, but she hated to see their spirit stifled. Bradley was a curious boy and she hoped his eagerness to learn never waned.

"Chief Harris knows all about them. You can ask him when you see him tomorrow." Cora smiled and saw a flicker of opportunity spark in Bradley's eyes. Amanda handed Cora a large opened envelope and Cora peeked inside before handing it to Mike Spicer. "Amanda made you some copies of the Spicer statue pictures for you to take home to the family."

"Thank you," Ellen said to Amanda as she took the photos from her husband and glanced through them.

"There's Rodney now." Cora pointed toward the lobby and Rodney waved.

"Good morning everyone," Rodney said shaking Mike Spicer's hand. "I'm Rodney Maddox, the one that called you. Is everyone ready to go?"

"We are," Mike said guiding his grandson out the door.

"Have a good time," Cora called out as they left Amanda's office and Ellen smiled as she followed the group out the door.

"Bradley is an inquisitive child," Amanda said smiling.

"A precocious mind is a teacher's dream," Cora said shutting her eyes with a smile of remembrance. "An early passion for learning should always be fueled."

"Did someone important say that?"

"Cora Mae Bingham!" Cora said laughing all the way back to her desk.

Sheri Richey

Chapter 12

"That's basically where we are," Conrad said as he glanced over at Wink who was sipping coffee from a travel mug.

"Have you talked to his doctor?"

"No, Alice ordered the records. I thought they'd respond quicker to her and she can decode them for me. I thought I would have an update from her yesterday, but I still don't know what was in that other pill bottle." Conrad turned the car at the stop light in Paxton. "I'm just going to drive by Tuttle's office first and see if he's there. Then we can head over to the garage."

"After we talked this morning, I called Max Littleton and asked him about the Buckeyes. He's a city cop here in Paxton. He said it's a chop shop. They've busted the place many times for selling stolen parts, but nothin' sticks. Charges get dismissed because whoever they claim bought the parts flies the coop. They couldn't tie anything to the owner."

"Figures it'd be dirty. It's a shady looking place," Conrad said slowing the car. "That's the accountant's office on the end." Conrad pointed to the last storefront on the strip mall. "It doesn't look like anyone's there."

"If he lives in Red River, can't you get Chief Fairmont to haul him in?"

"Something's up with that," Conrad said. "I've talked to Dan, but I don't think he's being straight with me. I think he's too close to the situation. He knew Booze pretty well and some of the things he told me don't add up."

"Hmm," Wink said as he squinted into the sun. Officer Harold Hobson was known to everyone in town as Wink because he had one eye that opened only halfway. He told everyone it was his good eye, but no one really knew if he was joking or not. "Well, I can put my two cents in," Wink said as he pulled sunglasses from the front pocket of his shirt. "Linda Sneedman is a gold digger with a daddy complex. I've peeled her off more than one old lap when we've raided the Wasabi in the past. She targets the old guys that brag about money. It's just her MO."

Conrad nodded.

"And maybe I'm biased, but I never knew no good to come from a group of bikers," Wink said with a sneer. "Now, there's nothin' wrong with riding a motorcycle. Did a bit of that as a young man myself, but when you meet a hoard of them all together, it usually spells trouble."

"From your dealings on night shift, I'm sure that's true," Conrad said turning the car down the road to the industrial park area. "The poker runs for charity that have come through town have all been decent people.

I've never had trouble from them, but I know what you mean."

Wink nodded and shifted in his seat. "This the place?"

Conrad pulled the car in the front lot of Sharpe Auto Service. "The bikes are on the side."

"This doesn't look so bad," Wink said lifting his sunglasses up.

"They've got a decent street storefront," Conrad agreed as he drove slowly through the crunching gravel and turned the corner to go around the building. "This is the biker's side."

"Hmm. Guess half of them ain't woke up yet," Wink said smiling. "There's only half a dozen or so here."

"That's what I was hoping for," Conrad admitted. "There were too many yesterday when I came by. I didn't expect a warm welcome."

Upon seeing the squad car approach, the bikers gathered near the open garage doors as Conrad and Wink stepped out of the car.

"Good morning gentlemen," Conrad said nodding. "I'm Chief Harris from Spicetown. This here is Officer Hobson. We'd like to ask you some questions about Booze Lockhart." Conrad could tell their shoulders relaxed slightly when he mentioned Booze's name. They had seemed prepared to resist at first but motioned him inside as they took seats scattered around the area.

"Go get Monty," an older heavyset biker with thinning hair said to a younger man dressed in a white t-shirt and jeans.

"I saw a few of you over in Spicetown last week and I know Booze had a financial interest in this place, so I'd hoped you could tell me a little about him." Rather than wait for the ringleader and to break the ice, Conrad decided to try to engage with the group.

"Yeah, we knew him," a man said from the door at the back of the work area. Walking out to join the group, Conrad recognized the man that had helped Kathy Lockhart move. "I'm Montana Black. This is my club. What do you want to know about Booze?"

"I assume you've heard that—"

"Yeah, we know he's dead. We didn't have nothin' to do with that." Montana stopped and put both hands in his pockets.

"Oh, I'm not insinuating that you did. I just thought you could tell me something about him. Was he involved in the business here?"

"Come on back," Montana said waving his hand at Conrad to follow. "Have a seat."

There was only one available chair across from a dirty metal desk and Conrad sat down in the small wood-paneled room. Wink planted himself in the doorway so he could see keep an eye on the garage and on Conrad.

"Booze invested in the place with Mel Sharpe. Mel runs the front." Montana leaned back in a wooden chair, lifting the front legs in the air.

"And you run the back?" Conrad asked.

"I keep an eye on things."

"But the business here in the back belonged to Booze?"

"He thought so," Montana said with a shrug. "He got a cut of things."

"So, he invested money and drew out profits? Did you do business with Booze?"

"You'd have to ask Mel. I don't know what he invested, but he paid us a cut for our work here."

"Oh, so you did work directly for Booze and he paid you and your guys?"

"That's the way it was supposed to work," Montana said as he let his chair legs fall to the floor.

"There were problems?"

"Sometimes," Montana paused as if he was considering explaining his statement, so Conrad waited, but Montana didn't say anything further.

"Look, I'm not here about how you do business or what kind of business goes on. This isn't my jurisdiction. I'm just here trying to figure out this guy, Booze. We don't know yet what went down exactly, and he seems to have a confusing back story. I'm trying to find out what kind of guy he was. That's all."

"Well, at first he seemed like a smart guy," Montana said hunching his shoulders. "Gonna make us a lot of money. We were all in."

Conrad nodded. "And later?"

"Turns out he's a thief and a liar. We were parting ways." Montana slapped his hands on the desk as if the conversation was over.

"And Kathy? Kathy Lockhart? You haven't parted ways with her." Conrad was taking a risk here and he saw Wink's head turn to glance at Montana.

"No, she wasn't part of the problem," Montana said as he glanced up at Wink and Conrad saw recognition cross Montana's face. Wink's eye being half closed made him memorable to people. Sometimes that was good. Other times, it was not an asset.

"Is she your investor now?"

"I guess so," Montana said smiling. "She'll get whatever Booze had. The divorce wasn't final."

"It looks like you're happy to do business with Kathy. I guess she isn't a thief and a liar?"

"No, she's not," Montana said as he pushed his fingers through his long black hair. "Booze never treated her right. Once all the legal stuff is settled, she's going to take care of this place."

"She told you that? She knows what needs to be done here to keep things going?"

"Well, she'll need our help. We're going to work with her."

"And Tuttle? You work with Stanford Tuttle, too?"

"No, that's Booze's guy. The two of them are the ones that rip everybody off."

"How so?"

"He's supposed to have all the money, see," Montana said leaning forward. "Except he always says he ain't got the money and can't pay. Booze says Tuttle has all his money and won't give it to him. You can't believe either one of them."

"So, Tuttle and Booze were trying to cheat you out of your share of the business. Kathy Lockhart is going to fix all that." Conrad was trying to make sense of Montana's vague explanation. He could only assume the business was selling stolen merchandise.

"Yeah."

"But if you were running the place, weren't you taking in the money initially? Wouldn't you be the one giving money to Booze instead of the other way around?"

"Nah," Montana said leaning back again in his chair. "We didn't handle any money here. We just did the work and expected to be paid our fair share. Simple as that."

"Okay," Conrad said standing. "I appreciate your time."

Montana just nodded as they left the office. Conrad and Wink walked back out into the open work area. Most of the men were lounging lazily while a few were working on their bikes, but all ignored them as they returned to their car.

After backing out of the parking area, Conrad turned around the building to the front entrance. "I think we should step inside the front here and see if Mel Sharpe is here. According to Paul Fairmont, Mel is an old school buddy of Booze's, so I might not be able to trust anything he says either, but it's worth a shot."

All the bays on the front of the building were busy. Cars were up on lifts and employees were working on repairs. The business looked legitimate from the street side. Conrad pulled open the entrance door next to the bays and saw an older woman standing behind a counter with a piece of paper in her hand looking at a computer monitor. Her hair had been dyed dark brown, but she had apparently decided not to continue that practice as there was at least an inch of gray showing on the top of her head.

"Good morning, Officers," she said smiling. "How can I help you?"

"We were hoping to speak with Mel Sharpe, if he's in," Conrad said smiling. Sensing her hesitation at what the right response should be, he continued. "It's about his friend, Booze Lockhart."

"Uh, I don't know. I don't know if he's here. Let me check and see."

Conrad and Wink wandered around the small dirty seating area. Red vinyl padded chairs with gapping splits exposing the cotton stuffing were not inviting, so they continued to pace the room at random.

"You think he's coming out?" Wink asked after they had waited several minutes.

"Maybe he's in the back talking to Montana first," Conrad said.

"Gotta get their stories straight," Wink muttered.

"Sorry, he's coming," the woman said as she walked back to the counter. "He's on the phone."

"Gentleman, how can I help you?" Mel Sharpe walked through the doorway behind the counter with an outstretched hand. He had a noticeable limp, dragging his left foot behind him with each step, but shook hands with Conrad and Wink vigorously.

"I'm Chief Harris from Spicetown and this is Officer Hobson. We wanted to ask you a few questions about Booze Lockhart."

"Sure," Mel said with enthusiasm. "Come on back and have a seat."

Conrad and Wink followed the uneven gait of Mel Sharpe as he limped down a poorly lit hallway to a large office with concrete block walls. "Can I get you some coffee?"

"No, thank you," Conrad said as he took a seat and Wink remained standing. Wink did not like to sit with his back to a door and waved off the invitation Mel gave to encourage him.

"So, I haven't seen Booze in a while. I heard that he passed away and I must admit it was a shock. We went to school together. We're the same age, you know. So, when you hear about someone your own age just up and dying by surprise, it makes you think, you know."

"Yes," Conrad said nodding. "Actually, we're here about the business. I understand Booze was an investor here?"

"I wouldn't call it that," Mel said scratching the unshaven whiskers on his chin. "Booze was an old friend. He helped me out a time or two. I helped him out when I could."

"So, he didn't get regular payments from your business? I was assuming there were profits from his investments." Conrad wanted Mel to think he knew more than he did, so he pulled out the folded paper in his breast pocket and studied it.

"Oh, that," Mel said leaning back. "No, I was just repaying an old loan. Booze was always good to me if I needed some help and I repaid him when I could. Just a friendly arrangement."

"So, he doesn't have any ownership here? There was never any paperwork signed between you and Booze?" Conrad pulled his reading glasses out of his other pocket and slipped them on.

"No, nothin' like that," Mel said rearranging things on his desk and avoiding Conrad's eyes.

"Was there a different arrangement for the motorcycle shop?"

"That's just a different part of my business. Montana Black runs that, and Booze was always interested in the bikes. He used to ride years ago, and he always wanted to check out what I had in there. Reminiscing about the past, you know."

"Hmm, so I guess Booze was well-off financially? If he helped you out with a loan, he was doing well?" Conrad raised his eyebrows and looked at Mel over the top of his reading glasses.

"Ah, I don't know about all that. He always seemed pretty set. I mean his daddy died and left him some land. I guess he was doing all right."

"Did Booze offer to invest in your business? I mean, he was going around telling everybody he owned part of this place, so I'm a little confused by your responses."

"You can't go by what Booze said. He was always bragging. He probably thought because I owed him a little money that he owned the place. He was just a blowhard. He wasn't serious."

"Do you know Stanford Tuttle?"

"Stan, sure. He's from Red River, too. Booze used him for taxes and such, I know. He works here in town somewhere."

"He doesn't handle your business or taxes?"

"Oh no," Mel said stretching back again in his chair. "Me and the wife take care of the books."

"Did you record Booze's loans in your books?" Conrad pulled his glasses off and stared at Mel. "Do you keep a record of that?"

"No, no," Mel said shaking his head. "It was just a friendly loan, personal loan, you know."

Conrad crossed his ankle over his other knee and put the note back in his pocket. "When was the last time you saw Booze Lockhart?"

"Ah, a couple of weeks ago maybe," Mel said frowning. "I think he dropped by one day. I couldn't tell you exactly."

"So, you only saw him when he dropped in?"

"Yeah, I don't get back to Red River anymore. I just saw him when he came by. Never knew when he was comin'."

"I guess you knew he was in the middle of a divorce," Conrad said.

"Yeah, that'd been going on for years. A sad thing." Mel shook his head and leaned forward on his elbows. "Sorry, I can't tell you much."

"How did you pay him?" Conrad could sense they had worn out their welcome.

"Pay him?"

"When you made these loan repayments, how did you pay him?"

"In cash," Mel said sitting up straight.

"So, you handed it to him when he came to visit you here at the shop?"

"No. Well," Mel stammered and squinted his eyes as if it pained him to explain. "Not directly."

Conrad raised his eyebrows in a silent request for explanation.

"I told him I had some money for him when he was here, but he always told me he'd send somebody over for it. I guess he didn't want to carry it around." Mel took a deep breath seeming satisfied with his answer.

"It was a large sum? Who did he send?" Conrad asked as he slipped his glasses back in his pocket.

"Depends. It was a few hundred usually. He wasn't used to carrying around a lot of cash."

"Who did he send?" Conrad saw hesitation as Mel's eyes shifted around the room and Conrad felt certain he was plotting a lie, so he gave him a nudge. "Was it Tuttle?"

"He came by a couple of times. I don't think he liked coming around though, so after that I just sent one of the guys over. Had him run it over to Tuttle's office."

"You must really trust your employees," Conrad said smiling. "Most people wouldn't give their employees a lot of cash to carry and expect them to come back."

Mel chuckled and relaxed. "I got some good guys here. Been with me for years. I guess maybe they know I'd come lookin' for them if they didn't."

"Thank you for your time," Conrad said standing. "Oh, one more thing, did Booze ever tell you about his health problems?"

"No, sir," Mel said shaking his head sadly. "I always thought he was fit as a fiddle. That's why his sudden death was such a shock."

"Okay," Conrad said stretching his arm out to shake Mel's hand. "You have a good day."

"You too," Mel called out as Conrad and Wink walked down the hallway to the front desk.

"Have a good day, ma'am," Conrad said to the woman who he assumed was Mrs. Sharpe as they passed by the front desk and out the door.

"Wow," Wink said slamming his car door shut. "That guy is a terrible liar."

Conrad chuckled. "He's so bad, we actually learned something."

"Yeah, looks like this Tuttle guy is up to his ears in it."

"Looks like it," Conrad agreed. "Let's swing by his office again and see if anyone showed up."

"Then we need to think about lunch," Wink said rubbing his stomach. "My tank is empty."

"Okay," Conrad laughed. Wink was a tall lanky guy who looked as starved as he claimed to be, yet he could eat twice the amount of any man Conrad had ever met.

"Wait," Conrad said before backing out of his parking spot. "It looks like I missed a call from the coroner." Conrad tapped his phone to call back and backed out as the phone rang through his car speaker.

"Connie!" Coroner Alice Warner answered the call on the first ring. "I just hung up from leaving you a voice message."

"Hey, Alice. I just saw I missed your call. Have you got something for me?"

"Have I ever! Have you got something to write with?"

"I'm driving, but Wink is here. Hang on a minute," Conrad pulled the paper from his pocket he had pretended to read to Mel Sharpe and passed it to Wink, who pulled a pen out of his pocket. "Okay, ready."

"I'm going to spell this for you," Alice warned. "O-L-A-N-Z-A-P-I-N-E, Olanzapine. That was the unmarked pills."

"What's that for?" Conrad asked as he glanced at the paper on Wink's knee.

"Most people know it by the brand name Zyprexa. It's an anti-psychotic used for schizophrenia and bipolar disorders, but mixed with Fluoxetine, the one he had the prescription for, it's used for major depressive disorders. What's interesting though is Booze didn't have any of that."

"So why did he have the prescription?"

"His medical records show a slight mention of situational depression, probably from stress or the divorce, but his primary health problem was early onset Alzheimer's Disease. He was just diagnosed about six months ago and his doctor noted that he came in his office shortly after that asking for Olanzapine. He told him it wasn't appropriate for his condition."

"Huh? Why would he ask for that?"

"There are some drug trials going on involving these two drugs in treating dementia-related psychosis and I'd guess he read them on the Internet. People are always reading something and asking their doctors to give them prescriptions for this thing or that."

"So, wait," Conrad said as he pulled the car into the parking lot of Tuttle's office and stopped. "The doctor did give him the Fluoxetine, right? Even if he didn't have any mental disorder?"

"Yes, but it was just for the depression. Fluoxetine is Prozac. I'm sure he didn't intend long term treatment. Booze didn't have any history of depression, but then again, learning you have Alzheimer's could be a factor. He might not have been handling that well."

"Okay," Conrad said taking a deep breath. "So, how'd he get it?"

"My guess would be he bought it off the street or got it from a friend. If you want something and you have some money, you can find anything."

"Are they dangerous when they're taken together?" Wink shouted. Wink had never grown accustomed to using the car's speaker for phone calls. He had Bluetooth in his car turned off and only used his cell phone, despite Conrad's warning he was taking a needless risk.

"No. In fact, they make a drug that is exactly those two combined because they are helpful for certain mental conditions, but they aren't safe for elderly dementia patients. Booze wasn't elderly, but he wasn't exhibiting severe symptoms of the Alzheimer's Disease yet. I agree with his doctor. It wasn't an appropriate treatment."

"But it didn't kill him?" Conrad said.

"Actually, in a roundabout way, I'd say it did. The autopsy shows he had a heart attack, but the drug levels in his tox results are more than triple what they should be."

"Suicide," Wink suggested.

"I'm not inclined that way," Alice said. "If you're going to commit suicide, you down the whole bottle. I'd lean towards accidental, but I'm not ready to write that down yet."

"What are the side effects of the drugs together?" Conrad asked.

"Exactly what you described of him. He would be dizzy, gaining weight, falling down. It might have even worsened memory problems for him, and he increased the medication himself to try to stop it. These are not drugs to self-medicate with when you don't know what you're doing."

"Well, until you write something down that stops me, I'm going to keep looking. I'd like to know where he got an anti-psychotic drug. Somebody has to know something about this. He didn't do all this on his own."

"The autopsy isn't done yet. He's still open on the table," Alice said as Wink cringed. "I'll let you know if anything else turns up."

"Thanks, Alice. Talk to you soon." Conrad tapped the button to disconnect the call and took a deep breath. "What do you think?"

"How much was in those bottles?" Wink asked.

"A lot," Conrad said. "There were thirty-six of the Zyprexa; an odd number to have. Most people start out with thirty or sixty, or maybe ninety."

"But if you buy it on the street, it could be any amount, I guess."

"I'm hoping I can get in his computer. Tabor is working on it and it might hold some answers. Let me call into the office and check on him." Conrad tapped the screen to call the office.

"I'm glad Tuttle isn't here," Wink said as the phone rang. "I'm hungry."

"Where do you want to eat?"

"Somewhere close," Wink said looking around the shopping plaza.

"Spicetown Police Department," Georgia Marks said as radios squawked in the background.

"Georgie, is Tabor around?"

"Yeah, he's right here, Chief. He got in your laptop. Let me transfer you to the desk."

Before Conrad could answer he heard a softer ring tone and Officer Eugene Tabor answered. "Hey, Chief! Did Georgie tell you we're in?"

"She did. Let me tell you what I'm looking for."

"Okay," Tabor said as Conrad heard papers rustling.

"I need any search results you find about Alzheimer's Disease, Zyprexa, Prozac, any kind of dementia treatment. Also keep an eye out for something that looks like he's trying to find someone to sell him Zyprexa on the street. He had some in his possession, but it wasn't prescribed for him. I'd like to know why he wanted it and where he got it."

"Got it, Chief."

"Also, anything on his finances like accounting software or business contracts. His income and investments are still a mystery. Anything involving his accountant, Stanford Tuttle."

"He's got a program on here for finances," Tabor said. "It's got a password on it, too. I'll try to get in."

"Okay, I'll check with you later."

"Wait, Chief," Tabor shouted. "Georgia…"

"Yeah?" Conrad could hear Georgia shouting something.

"Georgia says to tell you that Nellie Turner has come by again and wants to talk with you. She couldn't get anything out of her. And Ned Carey called. He asked that you call him back when you can. Nothing urgent."

"Okay, thanks." Conrad tapped the console button to disconnect the call. "Let's go eat."

"Yeah," Wink cheered, shaking his fist in the air as Conrad laughed.

Chapter 13

"Mayor?" Amanda said from Cora's doorway. "Nellie Turner is here."

Cora stifled a scowl and hit the save button on the draft of her speech. "You can send her in."

Nellie Turner peered cautiously around the door, leaning forward with her camera dangling from her neck.

"Come in, Nellie," Cora said cheerfully. "Have a seat." Cora couldn't remember ever seeing Nellie in City Hall.

"This is really pretty, Mrs. Bing. Look at all the books and the big table." Nellie's eyes roamed all around the room with obvious awe. "Was this Mr. Bing's room, too?"

"Yes, Nellie. It used to be his office."

"I've never been here before. Is it okay for me to be here?"

"Certainly," Cora said. "Where's Tommy?"

"Oh, he's outside. He didn't want to come in. He's waiting on me."

"Well, what can I do for you today?"

"Can I take a picture of your room?"

"Yes, you can. Are you still looking for the Chief?"

"Oh, yes. That's why I'm here. Do you know where he is?" Nellie held up her camera and scanned the room through the viewer.

"I think he had to go to Paxton today. Is there something I can help you with?"

"I need to talk to him."

"Well, he's really busy right now. Maybe once the holiday is over."

"I know he's working on that big case, the guy in the alley and I told him I would get him the pictures."

"You can leave them with me or at the police station. They'll get them to him as soon as he comes back to town."

"No, he has to come to my house. Tommy doesn't want me to take them anywhere."

"Oh, okay," Cora said bewildered. "I'll tell him if I see him. Are you going to the parade tomorrow?"

"Sure," Nellie said nodding her head forcefully. "I'm going to take pictures there, too."

"I'm sure I'll see you there. Did you get all the pictures you wanted?"

"No," Nellie said sadly. "I forgot. I can't really take any if Tommy's not here. Can I come back sometime? Maybe he'll come with me."

"Of course, you can. You can both stop by anytime."

"Thank you, Mrs. Bing. I'll go now," Nellie said as she walked backwards toward the door, glancing over her shoulder after every few steps. "You have a good day."

"You, too." Cora waved at her as she walked into Amanda's outer office area and heard sounds of Nellie bumping into chairs and Amanda mumbling until the office door finally shut. "Amanda?"

"Yeah?" Amanda came through the door with wide eyes. "Did you find out what she wants?"

"She just wants Conrad. Says he needs to come to her house so she can show him some pictures. I don't know," Cora said shaking her head. "Conrad always avoids Nellie. I think her awkwardness makes him uncomfortable. He'll not go willingly."

"Well, she'll not give up, so—"

"I know," Cora said smiling. "He needs to just suck it up and get it over with."

Amanda giggled.

"Can you grab that off the printer and read it over for me? Tell me what you think. It's just a draft and it doesn't feel right. I want your input."

"I'm not sure why you stress over these speeches," Amanda said picking the pages off the printer tray. "You never follow them after you write them. I've watched you give dozens of speeches and I know what they say before you get up there, but I never recognize them once you start talking."

"I know," Cora said shrugging. "I get distracted and start ad-libbing. I've always done that, but I need a foundation even if I don't follow it. It organizes my thoughts."

"Okay, but I wouldn't get too hung up on particular word choices when you're not likely to use them, anyway."

"That's good advice, but I can't help it. I'm driven."

Amanda chuckled as she walked back to her desk to read.

Before she could finish the first sentence, Amanda saw the Spicers walking across the lobby and toward her office. "Hi! Did you enjoy your tour?"

"We did, very much," Mike Spicer said as he peered into Cora's office. "We just wanted to thank the mayor and confirm what we were supposed to do tomorrow."

"Oh, a police car will pick you up at the Inn a little before eight o'clock tomorrow morning. I think it will probably be Officer Hobson, but it could be the Chief. They're both driving in the parade."

"Awesome," Bradley Spicer said.

"When the parade ends, you'll all go with the mayor to the statue and there will be seats there for you. Did you get a look at the statue today?"

"We did," Ellen Spicer said. "It's really beautiful."

Amanda smiled. "After the dedication ceremony, you'll have free time to look around the fair at Market Days. There will be food vendors there as well as local craftsmen and produce stands. Lots of things to look at and try out."

"That sounds like a lovely day," Ellen said. "What time are the fireworks?"

"They'll be at nine o'clock, and if at any point you are ready to go back to the Inn, just look for someone wearing one of these armbands." Amanda held up one to show them what the Spicetown Security band looked like. "They'll radio the station, and someone will come give you a lift back. If you don't see anyone handy, just call the station and they'll send a car."

"Sounds great," Mike Spicer said as he patted his grandson, Bradley, on the back. "We'll get out of your way now and see you sometime tomorrow. Thank you for everything and be sure and thank the mayor for us, too."

"I will." Amanda smiled as she heard them thanking Rodney for the tour just outside her office door before walking through the lobby.

Rodney looked in the door at Amanda and grinned. "I think everything went well. We had a good time." Rodney gave her a thumbs up sign.

"I'll let the mayor know. That was really a nice thing you did, offering to show them around. They're a nice family and that grandson is something else."

"Yeah, he's a hoot. He made it fun for me, asking a million questions and telling stories. He's a great kid. See you tomorrow."

Amanda sat down at her desk to read through the mayor's speech and found herself giggling after the first paragraph. If the mayor actually kept to the speech she'd written, the fireworks might actually begin much earlier than nine o'clock.

"I think I'm going to get Asher to go pull Tuttle for me," Conrad said as he slowed the car's speed to enter the Spicetown city limits. "You've got to be at City Hall at five o'clock and I don't have time to drive around Red

River hunting Stanford Tuttle tonight. I've got to write up these reports and I want to check on that laptop."

"You could have Dan Fairmont bring him over," Wink suggested.

"I don't think I want to involve him. I'll have Georgie call over there and give him a heads up about the time Asher reaches Red River, but I don't want to give him any more warning than that. I'm not sure he's not hiding Tuttle from me. I hate it, but I don't feel good about it, the way things stand."

"I can run over there after I do the security detail briefing, if you want."

"That's okay. Asher can handle it and it will get him out from under foot for an hour," Conrad said chuckling. Officer Roy Asher had a tendency to hang around the station more than he should. "You've got about an hour and a half though. Can you make some calls for me?"

"Sure," Wink said. "What do you need?"

"I haven't reached out to Kathy Lockhart's attorney yet. Tanner Buckley handled her divorce and he might want to cough up whatever financial information he found on Booze. Kathy said that was what was holding everything up. Booze wasn't disclosing his assets when the judge asked for them and it kept causing delays. I'm sure Buckley had somebody looking into all that."

"I can do that."

"Oh, I have a bunch of papers I found at the Red River Ranch I haven't gone through yet either. I flipped through them a little last night, but I need to read them. He had them hidden in his room so they must be something important." Conrad pulled his car into the parking place by the side door of the PD that was reserved for him. "Let's go see what Tabor found."

Conrad walked into the dispatch office and paused. Georgia Marks had her back to him talking on the phone. Eugene Tabor was hunched over a computer monitor squinting and scrolling with his index finger flying over the mouse.

Roy Asher wasn't parked in a visitor chair filling his face with twinkies or french fries as usual and no one even noticed he was there. He put his hands on his hips and waited.

Wink walked up behind him and stopped. "Is this what day shift is like? I don't think I like it."

"Oh, hey Chief," Tabor said glancing up briefly. "I got some good stuff here."

"Chief!" Georgia planted her rubber-soled shoes firmly on the linoleum floor and pushed off, so her chair rolled out the entrance of the dispatch cubicle. "I'm glad to see you. We got a situation."

"Glad to be seen," Conrad huffed. "What's going on?"

"Mabel Williams just called. She said the Turner house got broken into. They don't have a phone, so she called it in. I sent Darren Hudson over there, but you know Nellie Turner is going to want you."

"I've got a lot on my plate right now. Do we know if anything was taken?"

Before Georgia could answer, the radio called her back, so she pushed off the floor again to roll back inside the dispatch booth.

Wink crossed the room and sat down at an empty desk, clicking on a laptop. "I'm going to see if I can reach Tanner Buckley before it gets too late."

"Okay," Conrad said nodding and then turned toward dispatch. Picking up a little of the conversation, he thought Officer Hudson was talking about Nellie's house.

"That was Hudson," Georgia said swiveling her chair back around. "He said it's hard to tell what's missing because the house was trashed. The TV is gone though. He knows that much. He's asking for help to print the area. You want me to send Asher?"

"No, I need Asher to run to Red River for me," Conrad said turning his head to look around the office. "Where is Asher?"

"He's on patrol," Georgia said.

Conrad chuckled. He thought Asher only did that when he made him. "Call him and tell him to go to Red River and see if he can pick up Stanford Tuttle at his house. I need to interview him, and he's been avoiding me. I need you to give Red River PD a heads up but wait until Asher is just about hitting the city limits."

"Okay, Chief," Georgia said making notes on the pad she kept by the phone. "You want Tabor to go to Nellie Turner's?"

"Ugh, No," Conrad said scowling. "I need him to keep working on that laptop. I guess I'll go. She's not going to be happy until I talk to her, anyway." Conrad spun around on his heels and started down the hallway towards the side door.

"She's been by here twice today," Georgia hollered, and Conrad just waved his hand as he pushed the side door open.

As soon as Conrad started his car, he tapped the screen to select Cora's cell phone number and heard the phone begin to ring as he backed the car out.

"Hey, Connie. Busy day?"

"Sure is. I finally heard from Alice on the mystery drugs. Do you know anything about Prozac or Zyprexa? Apparently, he had both, but only one was prescribed."

"I know Prozac is for depression and Zyprexa is for a more serious mental condition, but nothing specific," Cora said. "Before I forget, Nellie Turner has been by City Hall twice today looking for you."

"I'm headed out there now. She's been by the station, too, but we've got a reported break-in out there now."

"A break-in," Cora said with a gasp. "Why would anyone try to steal from those two? They're barely getting by. They don't have anything to steal."

"Hudson is out there now, and he said the TV is gone and the place is trashed. I'm going out to help."

"I've got some time. I'll run out there and help with Nellie. She's going to be climbing all over everyone. She's just had that TV a few months. Shelby at the flea market gave it to her for free and she was over the moon about it. She thinks she can talk to the President on it."

"The President of the United States?" Conrad shouted. "Good grief, Cora. Yes, maybe you need to come out there because I don't do well with crazy. You know that."

"Nellie isn't crazy," Cora scolded. "She's—"

"Anyone talking to the President of the United States through an old TV—"

"Connie, stop fighting it. Nellie's very easy to talk to if you just go with the flow. Be agreeable and accepting. She has a very kind heart."

Conrad's chest raised with an audible sigh. "How soon can you be there?"

Cora Mae giggled. "I'm leaving right now."

Conrad smiled and shook his head. Cora Mae could tame a rabid bear, but she could also become one if you crossed her.

Tapping the console again, the phone dialed Ned Carey. Conrad had almost forgotten about Georgia giving him that message.

"Hey, Connie."

"Hey, Ned. Georgie said you called earlier?"

"Yeah, I know you're busy, but I got to thinking after we talked about Booze."

"You remembered something?"

"Yeah, I knew I'd done a little digging on him after he first stopped by my office. I was curious about him and I made some notes. It took a little bit to find them, but I've got a list of places he owns or has some financial connection with, if that would be helpful to you."

"Yes, I'd like to see it. I'm driving right now. Can you email it to me?"

"Sure thing," Ned said. "I won't keep you. See you tomorrow."

"Okay, thanks." Conrad said tapping the button to disconnect as he pulled his car slowly off of Rosemary Road and through the grass in front of Nellie Turner's home. It was a small wood-framed house badly in need of a coat of paint but there was no driveway because the Turners didn't have a car. Cora had told him Nellie's mother had lived here and both of her children, Nellie, and Tommy, were raised here. Neither of them ever left home.

Conrad saw Tommy sitting slumped over against the side of the house on a stack of concrete blocks, but he didn't look up when Conrad closed the car door.

"Chief! Chief!" Glancing over at the sound of Nellie's voice, Conrad saw her high stepping through the tall weeds alongside the road in a frenzied effort to get to him. Darren Hudson stood in the front doorway with gloved hands holding his camera. Conrad nodded hello to Darren and waited for Nellie to reach him.

"Are you okay, Miss Turner?"

"Yes, Chief. I had to go to Miss Williams' house to ask her to call you and she wanted me to wait there, but I saw your car go by."

"I came to help Officer Hudson. Are you and your brother all right?"

"Yes, but they took my camera and our TV. It's a mess. My front door is broken now. They threw things everywhere. How could someone come in our house like that? That's so rude."

"I agree. It's not right. The mayor is on her way out here to see you. I told her what happened, and she wanted to come check on you. Can you wait out here for her? I need to go inside your house with Officer Hudson."

"Okay. Okay. I didn't touch anything. I promise. Miss Georgia told me not to and I didn't. Tommy didn't either." Nellie was breathless from her rapid speech and her jaunt to the neighbor's house.

"That's good. Let me see what we can do. Just wait here," Conrad said holding up his hands in hopes she would stay calm and still. Tommy remained slouched in a glum silence on the side of the house and didn't acknowledge either of them.

Conrad stepped carefully through the front door and examined the damage on the door jamb. The wood frame was softened with age and would not have offered much resistance to a strong shoulder or a simple pry bar. Pulling on latex gloves he glanced around the disheveled front room. Cushions from the sagging sofa were flipped over with papers strewn across the floor. Stepping through the living area, he saw a small kitchen in the back of the house with all six cabinet doors open. All the contents were pushed out onto the floor.

"Chief," Darren Hudson hollered from the side bedroom. "Chief, I think there's something in here you need to see."

Stepping carefully around the littered floor, Conrad turned into the small bedroom. With a twin mattress on the floor in the corner, the rest of the room was bare except for the walls. The walls were covered with penciled drawings on yellowing paper held to the wall with thumb tacks.

"Chief, over here," Hudson said motioning Conrad to come to the corner near the mattress. "Isn't this your dead guy?"

"Huh?" Conrad leaned in and pulled his reading glasses from his pocket. Sliding them up as he bent over, he marveled at the artistry of the drawings. They were amazingly lifelike and detailed. "Holy cow!"

"I know," Hudson said with wide eyes. "Incredible, isn't it? These are fantastic. There's a bunch here of you, too."

"They are impressive," Conrad said straightening his back and looking at the surrounding pictures. Sliding his phone from his pocket, he took a couple of close-up shots of some of the drawings. "I think I need to talk to Nellie."

Officer Hudson nodded when Conrad turned to go. Stepping across the front door threshold gingerly, Conrad looked out and saw Cora Mae standing there alone.

"Hey there," Conrad said. "Where's Nellie?"

"She's talking to Tommy. He's having a hard time with all of this," Cora said as lines creased her forehead. "Once you are done here, I'm going to get someone out here to replace their front door. Would it be all right if they came out now and measured? I don't want them to have nowhere to sleep tonight."

"Sure. I'm going to print it now and Hudson has already gotten photos."

"Rodney Maddox is off work today and if I can reach him, I'm sure he'd be happy to help." Cora pulled her phone from her jacket pocket.

"I'll start with that now and then they can do whatever needs to be done. Take a look at these," Conrad said as he held out his phone turned sideways and brushed his finger across the screen to display the shots he'd taken inside of the drawings.

"That's Booze," Cora said breathlessly. Conrad stroked his finger to turn to the next picture. "Oh, that's us!" Cora chuckled at seeing the picture Conrad had been forced to pose for on the street corner a few days before. "Connie, these are really good. You think she knows Booze?"

"I don't know, but she definitely has seen him before." Conrad looked down at the closeup of Booze's face. A cigarette was poised between his fingers and he was either raising or lowering the cigarette, but the facial lines, the brow, and the expression were so sharp, it was clearly Booze Lockhart.

Cora walked to peer around the side of the house. "Nellie, dear. Can you come here for just a minute?"

Nellie nodded and hurried over to Cora's side.

"Nellie, the Chief was just inside your house and took some pictures." Cora pulled Nellie closer and pointed at Conrad's phone. "Did you draw these?"

"Wow, that's my picture on your phone," Nellie said beaming.

"Yes, but did you draw that?" Cora pointed again as Conrad held the phone out.

"I took that picture in the alley that night. I told you," Nellie said turning to Conrad. "Tommy, he develops them for me. He was all done with them, but he wouldn't let me take them to town to show you. I was trying to tell you that you'd have to come to my house because Tommy wanted them to stay here."

"Ah," Conrad said looking up through the trees. "That's why you came by the station today?"

"Yes, I wanted to tell you that," Nellie said and then pointed at the front door of the house. "There's more in there. The man in the alley, the motorcycles, I took lots of pictures that day."

"Okay, I'll go look at the others," Conrad said with a knowing glance at Cora.

"Be right back," Nellie said as she scurried over to her brother's side again.

"She's still got that camera hanging around her neck and it's possible someone turned over her house looking for the camera or the pictures she took."

"You think? Oh my. This is going to put her and Tommy in danger," Cora said wincing. "She's not going to turn loose of that camera either."

"Well, running around town all the time snapping all these imaginary pictures and then telling everybody she's got photos of them…" Conrad shook his head in frustration. "Geeze."

"I know." Cora's shoulders slumped. "But she doesn't mean any harm and it makes her happy. Everyone in Spicetown knows she's harmless. That means this wasn't done by someone from Spicetown."

Conrad frowned in frustration. "Let me get back inside. I'd like to take these pictures but I'm sure Tommy will have a meltdown, so I'll just photograph them for now."

"I think that's best." Cora looked down at her phone and hit the speed dial for her office.

"Mayor Bingham's office. Can I help you?"

"Mandy, it's Cora. Can you try to reach Rodney Maddox for me? Nellie and Tommy Turner have had a break-in at their house, and someone destroyed their front door. I need to find someone to come out today and measure the doorway for a new frame and door. I know Rodney does some handyman work. Can you ask him if he's free right now and would like to come do this for me? Of course, I'll pay him but if he isn't available, see if he knows someone we can call. This can't be left overnight."

"Wow. Okay. Yes, I can call him. He's off all day and he'll probably do it if I can catch him. Were they robbed?"

"They lost a few things, yes, but bless their hearts, they don't have much. I've got to make sure they at least have a safe place to stay tonight."

"I'll call him right now."

"Tell him they'll need a new doorknob and a deadbolt lock, too."

"I will."

"Thank you. I'll wait to hear from you," Cora said as she tapped her phone off and watched Nellie stroke Tommy's arm soothingly. She didn't imagine Tommy could handle a night away from home, and the Nutmeg Inn was likely full of holiday guests, anyway.

"Chief?" Hudson was in the kitchen dusting the cabinets for prints.

"Yeah, I'm here." Conrad yelled out and then looked in the kitchen. "Turns out Tommy is the artist. I'm not going to ask to take the pictures down, but I'm going to go in there and get some more photos. Are you finding anything?"

"Lots of prints here but I'm sure they probably belong to the Turners."

"Yeah and I don't know if I can get them to give me their prints to exclude. It's worth collecting, but I don't see we can do much with them right now, unless we get a suspect."

"I'm done with Tommy's room and almost done here in the kitchen."

"I'm going to dust the front door now. The mayor is sending somebody out to replace it for them so they're secure tonight."

"Okay, Chief. I'll do the living room next."

"I'll do Nellie's room and then I've got to get back to the office. Can you canvas the neighbors when you're done? Asher should be back in about an hour and I'll send him to help."

"Sure thing," Hudson said as he leaned over the kitchen table to label the print card.

Conrad walked out to his car to get his fingerprint kit and saw Cora on the side of the house talking with Nellie and her brother, Tommy.

Sheri Richey

Chapter 14

"Can I help you?" Stanford Tuttle opened the front door to his house cautiously and peered out.

"Officer Asher here," Roy Asher said as he tugged up his leather belt that kept slipping below his stomach. "I'm from the Spicetown Police Department and the Chief sent me. He'd like to speak with you and I'm here to drive you over to the station."

"I'm sorry," Tuttle said feigning confusion.

"You are Stanford Tuttle," Asher said for clarification, although he'd already looked at the driver's license photo and knew the answer.

"I am."

"Chief Harris would like to talk with you regarding the death of your friend, Booze Lockhart."

"We were just business associates," Tuttle stammered with a frown.

"Nevertheless, he has tried several times to reach you and it's urgent that he speak with you."

"What could be so urgent? It's late in the day. I don't want to travel all the way to Spicetown now. Can't I just make an appointment to see—"

"My instructions are to bring you, sir. We'll give you a ride home after." Asher was going to try the diplomatic method first. The Chief always told him he jumped on people too quick. It seemed to work for Chief Harris, but in Asher's experience, a strong arm was faster.

"Give me a few minutes," Tuttle said starting to close the door. "I need to change clothes."

Asher nodded, but he suspected Tuttle was running to his phone and not his closet. Roy pulled out his cell phone and texted a message to Georgia in dispatch that Tuttle was home, and he was waiting on him. He didn't want to leave the front porch to go back to his car radio.

After several minutes, Asher jumped when he heard the automatic garage door open. Running to the driveway, he had to jump aside as Tuttle backed out. Asher slammed the palm on his hand against the driver's side window as it passed by and Tuttle stopped the car. The automatic window rolled down.

"I'm sorry, Officer. I didn't mean to startle you."

Channeling the Chief, Roy took a deep breath. "There's no need for you to drive over there. I'm happy to give you a ride."

"Thank you," Tuttle said an aloof glance. "I prefer to drive myself."

"Okay," Roy said as he walked away muttering to himself. "Suit yourself."

Settling in the car, he saw Tuttle back out and had to hurry to turn around in the drive to tail him. Once they were out of Red River and on the highway, he contacted Georgia in dispatch again.

"Georgie, I'm following Tuttle now. He won't ride in the squad so let's hope he knows the way."

"Okay, I'll let the Chief know."

§

"Oh, Rodney," Cora said with her hands clasped under her chin. "You're a lifesaver. I'm so glad you were able to come."

"Happy to help, Mayor," Rodney said offering his hand to Cora to shake. "I brought my old front door. If it fits, this won't take long. I just need to measure it."

"Your door?"

"Yeah, it was just leaning in the back of the garage and I hadn't done anything with it. Carmen wanted one of those fancy beveled glass doors on the front, so I took down our old door and put it in garage last fall. I don't need it for anything and it's a perfectly good door. No reason not to put it to use if it's the right size. It's over there in the back of my truck."

"That's wonderful. Thank you."

"Is it okay for me to go up there and check it out?"

"Yes, the Chief said he's all done with it and I told him you were coming."

While Rodney measured, Cora Mae walked over to Rodney's truck and looked at the door. It was aluminum paneled and even had a peep hole in it. The doorknob and deadbolt were still installed with the keys dangling from the lock. She crossed her fingers it would be a good fit.

"The size is okay," Rodney said walking back to his truck and propping his elbow up over the tailgate. "The real problem is that all the wood is soft. There's lots of wood rot because it hasn't been painted enough to seal the wood from moisture. I can't promise someone won't push this door in, too."

"The Chief had the same concern, but at least the door jamb will be in good shape and the metal door will make it harder for someone to get in. I haven't walked around the back to see what shape the back door is in yet. Just do the best you can."

Rodney nodded and put the tailgate of his truck down to slide out his large metal toolbox.

"Nellie," Cora called out and waved. "Can you come here for a minute?"

Nellie was sitting on the stack of concrete blocks in the shade beside her brother and popped up when she heard her name. Jogging up to the truck, she smiled at Rodney.

"Nellie, this is Rodney and he's going to put this door up for you."

"Hi, Rodney."

"Miss Turner," Rodney said with a smiling nod as he turned to carry his toolbox to the front steps.

"Now, when he's done, he's going to give you some keys to the door. This door has two locks on it but the key works for both of them. When you're inside, there is a little lever you turn on the doorknob to lock the bottom and a bigger lever above that. You need to be sure and turn both of those to lock the door well when you're inside."

"My old door has the thing on the doorknob," Nellie said nodding.

"Yes, this will have that plus an extra bigger lock called a deadbolt. When he's done, Rodney will show you how to lock them on the inside, but when you and Tommy go somewhere, you must lock the house up with the keys. Always carry the keys with you and then you can get back inside when you come home."

"I have keys," Nellie said digging into her jeans pocket.

"The keys to the old door won't work anymore. You'll have new keys now, but you know how to do all that, right?"

"Yes, I can unlock the door with the key."

"Does your back-door lock?" Cora had a sinking feeling that fixing the front door was only a small drop in the bucket of the many repairs that were needed.

"No, but we don't use it."

Cora frowned. "Is the back left unlocked all the time?"

"Yes," Nellie said nodding. "I don't have any keys for that door."

"Oh, goodness," Cora said mostly to herself. "We can't have that. Maybe we can have keys made for it."

Conrad stepped through the front door after talking with Rodney and saw Cora waving him over.

"Chief, did you check the back door? Nellie says it isn't locked."

"They can't use the back door," Conrad said glancing quickly at Cora and shaking his head. "It should be okay for now."

"Well, okay," Cora said warily. "If you have any questions, you need to ask Rodney, okay?"

"Okay, I will," Nellie said as she skipped back to her seat in the shade.

"The refrigerator is sitting in front of the back door," Conrad said softly. "They can't get in or out of it."

"Mercy," Cora said. "What if there's a fire? That's not safe."

"I know but the kitchen is tiny, and the house was probably built before refrigerators got so big. There's really no where to put it unless you tear out cabinets."

"This just really isn't suitable for anyone to live in," Cora said shaking her head in a rage.

"Now before you go taking on another project to save the world, let me remind you that these kids grew up here and have never lived anywhere else. They wouldn't want to move even if you bought them the Taj Mahal, so you don't even need to put this on your list."

Cora sneered mockingly at Conrad but couldn't argue with his point. "Maybe it just needs some work."

"Oh boy, that's an understatement," Conrad muttered. "It needs to be leveled, but I don't think they'd ever go for that."

"Maybe a trailer," Cora said with a head tilt. "If I could show them a mobile home and get them comfortable with that, we could tear down this house and put the trailer on this land."

"Don't go sayin' *we*. I've got a full-time job that needs doin' and I'm not looking for a project."

"Oh, Connie. Don't be selfish. These folks need help and we could help them."

"I'm going to help them. I'm going to help them by getting back to work. I've got an interview coming in and I need to be back at the station. Hudson is finishing up."

"I'm going back to the office, too. I need to see Amanda before she leaves for the day and the volunteers will be showing up soon. Rodney can take care of this. Who's coming in?"

"Stanford Tuttle is on his way over with Asher on his tail. He wouldn't ride with Asher so he's following him in from Red River. They're about fifteen minutes out right now."

"If I don't hear from you, I'll see you in the morning," Cora said as she walked toward Rodney to give him last instructions.

§

"Hey, Roy," Conrad said when Asher answered his phone.

"Chief, I'm still about eight to ten minutes out."

"That's okay. I just got back in the office. How'd it go at Tuttle's house?"

"He didn't exactly invite me inside, if that's what you mean."

"Why didn't he just ride with you?"

"No idea," Roy shouted. "He looked me up and down like I was a dead racoon and then put his nose in the air. Said he had to go change his clothes first, but he's wearing the same thing. I'm sure he made a phone call, and somebody told him not to get in my car."

"You think everybody's heard about how bad you drive?" Conrad choked on his laughter. "Maybe he's afraid for his life."

"Ah, Chief," Roy whined. "I ain't that bad."

"You're just used to it. So, what do you think about this guy?"

"Pretty uppity, if you ask me. Has his little loafers on and drives his fancy car. Wanted to just make an appointment because he thought it was too late in the day." Asher said in a theatrical falsetto.

"Did you tell him how sorry we were to inconvenience him?"

"I told him it was urgent and that you'd been trying to reach him. He didn't admit to knowing that though. He said Booze isn't his friend. He was a business associate."

"Hmm, well, let's hope he actually shows up," Conrad said as he clicked on his computer and opened his email.

"Oh, he better go straight there," Roy warned. "I'm prepared to chase him down if he don't, and I think he knows that."

Conrad chuckled at Roy's bravado. "Okay, I'll see you soon."

Conrad clicked to open Ned's email and saw a quick note explaining Booze was linked to these businesses and he had more details on the companies if Conrad needed it. Some were familiar to Conrad like the Wasabi and Sharpe's Auto, but the Paxton Fitness Depot and the Concord Car Wash in Paxton were new leads. Ned closed by saying that Stanford Tuttle was also an investor in these businesses and that gave Conrad a good place to start.

§

Cora heard the roar of conversation in the lobby of City Hall and checked the clock on her computer screen. It was time to start the briefing. Walking out her office door, she spotted Harvey Salzman and smiled. Saucy, as everyone called him, was a dedicated crime stopper in Spicetown and she wasn't surprised to see he had volunteered for the security detail, despite his advanced age.

"Hey, Saucy. Did you sign up for the security detail?"

"Sure did, Mayor. I saw in the paper you needed help and you know I'm always willing to help this town."

"I know you are, Saucy, and I appreciate that very much."

"I told Miss Amanda that I would work in the afternoon when the fair is going on. I like to watch the parade and I'm not cut out for night duty," Saucy said shaking his head in regret. "I'm not fond of firecrackers and I need to be home with my little dog. That noise is so scary for her. I don't want her to be alone."

"I love to watch parades, too. And I think it's wise for you to stay away from fireworks," Cora said with a smiling wink. Saucy nodded his head shyly and joined the crowd as Wink began to talk.

"Quiet down," Wink yelled to the crowd milling about the lobby of City Hall and silence settled in. "Go ahead, Mayor."

"Welcome everyone," Cora said smiling to the crowd. "I can't tell you how heartwarming it was for me when I heard we had so many citizens willing to step up in our time of need." Cora placed her palms together under her chin and smiled. "I want to thank each and every one of you for being willing to give up some of your holiday time, time you should be enjoying your town, just to watch over others. When the City Council abruptly cut the holiday funding without notice and our ability to pay for the holiday security detail was ripped out from under us, initially we panicked, and I had to reach out to our citizens. I apologize for this burden, but I think we have the best of Spicetown gathered right here today." Cora paused a moment for the group applause to settle. "I won't keep you. Here is your coach and leader, Officer Hobson."

"Hello, everyone. Miss Morgan is going to pass out armbands to each of you. These have to be worn during your shift so folks can identify you if they need help. Before you leave today, I need for you to make certain Miss Morgan has your cell number on her list and that you have that cell phone on your person during your shift. Communication is important."

Amanda wandered through the standing crowd and handed arm bands to each person as Wink talked and Cora slipped quietly back into her office.

Picking up her phone from her desk, she called the Old Thyme Italian Restaurant across the street and spoke with the owner's daughter, Jo Biglioni.

"Hi, Jo. This is Cora Mae. Can you make up about five large pizzas for me? I'm going to take them over to the police station. Just a mix of things, whatever you think they'd like."

"Sure can. It'll be about thirty minutes or so."

"That's fine. Conrad is going to be working through dinner and he gets grumpy when he doesn't eat," Cora said laughing.

"We'll take care of it, Mayor," Jo said. "Good luck with the parade tomorrow."

"Thank you. I'll be looking for you."

"Oh, I'll be there," Jo said chuckling as she hung up the phone.

Sheri Richey

Chapter 15

Conrad glanced through his email and Wink's name caught his eye. Wink rarely sent emails but then again, he spent very little time in the office on night shift. The subject line indicated it was the information he had gathered from Kathy's attorney.

> Chief,
>
> Talked to Buckley and boy does he hate Booze! Says he's sneaky, underhanded and one of the best liars he's ever met. Anyway, he said at first he thought Booze was hiding money in investments but after some digging, he decided the guy is flat broke. Says he's just a con man and a bully. Makes people put his name on their business by promising them money or he blackmails them into it. Then he lives off the profit and hush money they pay him. He can't prove it, but he can't find any real dough either. Told me to talk to the Concord Car Wash guy. That guy is the one he got most of his info from.

Asked him about Tuttle too. He said he's pretty sure he's embezzled Booze's money. Again, he can't prove it. Tuttle says the money is gone, but Tuttle's bank account is growing. Buckley had him tailed for a week with a PI and he doesn't even have any real business. Said he didn't see a single customer. The storefront is a sham. All of Booze's businesses have Tuttle's name on them too. The gym in Paxton is all Tuttle's now and he owns 51% of the car wash. Buckley thinks Booze strong arms his way into the businesses and then Tuttle takes over Booze's position. Booze doesn't even know what's going on. He trusts Tuttle.

Buckley said Kathy told him that Tuttle gives Booze money whenever he wants, and Buckley thinks that's what kept Booze quiet. Tuttle just told him he had money and he believed him. Bottom line - Tuttle stole it all.

Just speculation but thought you'd want to know before you talk to him.

Wink

"Chief?" Conrad jumped at the sound of Officer Asher's voice. He had been deep in thought over the information from Ned Carey and Wink.
"Yeah, Roy? Is he here?"
"I put him in an interview room for you."
"Good. Thanks. Can you check on Hudson for me? He was out at Nellie Turner's house and he may need

help with a neighborhood canvas. I had to leave before he finished."

"Sure, Chief," Asher said hiking his leather belt up again. "I'll radio and see if he needs help."

"Is Tabor still around?"

"Yeah, he's out front with his nose in that laptop."

"Okay, I need to check with him before I go in there." Conrad stood and shut his email.

"Good luck in there, Chief," Asher said as he walked down the hallway.

"Is the Chief still in there?" Tabor asked Asher as they passed in the hallway and Asher nodded. "Chief?"

"Yeah, Tabor. I'm here."

"Chief, you need to see this before you go in there." Tabor ran around the side of Conrad's desk and started fanning out pages he had printed from the laptop. "Here is an email where Booze asked Tuttle to get him those pills."

"Excellent, Tabor," Conrad said grinning. His intuition had been right this time.

"And these," Tabor tapped on the next two pages. "These are Booze telling Tuttle that he knows Tuttle is stealing his money."

"So, Tuttle was in the hot seat with Booze. Hmm," Conrad said reclining in his chair. "What about the financials?"

"I can't get in that program. It's password protected and I'm still working on it, but it's not the same password as the email and laptop."

"Great, job. This is great. Thank you." Conrad grabbed a stack of folders along with Tabor's emails and followed him down the hall. "Let me know if Wink comes back in."

"Sure thing, Chief."

Conrad looked in the window of the interview room before opening the door and saw Stanford Tuttle resting calmly. He was a slight man with a pale pasty complexion and wire-framed glasses. Although he had noticeably thinning brown hair on the top of his head, his arms were covered with thick dark hair that looked long enough to require combing. He had expected to see some anxiety based on what Ned Carey had said about his court testimony, but he looked quite content, almost serene. Conrad put his hand on the doorknob and decided that he would start by shaking that confidence.

"Evening, Mr. Tuttle. I'm Chief Harris." Conrad stretched out his hand to shake and Tuttle nodded his head in greeting but did not return the handshake.

"Good evening, Chief. Nothing personal, but I prefer not to shake hands."

"That's quite all right, Mr. Tuttle. I appreciate you coming into the office for me. I've been to your office a few times, but it was closed."

"Yes, well," Tuttle stammered and looked over at the corner of the desk. "My secretary is on vacation, so I just decided to close this week."

"It's a holiday week. Popular time to be off." Conrad pulled out a chair across from Stanford Tuttle and crossed one ankle over his knee to put his papers in his lap. Lifting the top sheet, he shifted through the papers and rearranged a few to pass the time.

"Mr. Tuttle, I understand that you were a financial manager for Booze Lockhart. Is that true?"

"I handled some of his business affairs. Taxes, etcetera."

"And you two were friends?"

"No, just business associates." Tuttle glanced away to the table's edge again and Conrad made a mental note of this subtle tell.

"Do you think Booze felt that way, too?"

"I don't know what you mean," Tuttle said haughtily, raising his chin in the air.

"I mean, if Booze were alive and he was asked, would he have considered you his friend?"

"I have no idea," Tuttle said shaking his head and shrugging his shoulders at the same time.

"Well, I hear that you both grew up in Red River and other people consider you a friend to Booze, as well as a business associate. I'm figuring you know a little about both sides of the man, business and personal."

"I am fairly well versed in his business interactions. Nothing more."

"So, you were aware that he forced his way into existing businesses with false promises of investment?" Conrad raised an eyebrow in anticipation of Tuttle's denial.

"I was aware of his tactics. They are not a reflection on how I do business, however."

"I see," Conrad said squinting his eyes. "So, when Booze started accusing you of embezzling his funds, you assumed it was another tactic of his? Or did you realize that he was not as stupid as you thought he was?"

"It was merely his nature. He did not handle loss well and he lashed out. Investments sometimes lose money."

"Oh, so Booze was just blowing off steam when he made those accusations?" Conrad smiled as he saw redness begin to creep up Tuttle's neck. He was making a concerted effort to appear poised, but his body language was failing him.

"Exactly. It's not uncommon."

"Well, I'm not investigating allegations of financial crimes here, unless it reflects a motive, however I am still a bit unclear on the extent of your relationship with him. Based on comments from others that knew him well, reading emails that passed between you two and other material on his laptop, I am convinced that he considered you a close confidante, whether you felt a friendship existed or not."

Tuttle stared at the corner of the room and Conrad let the silence take a few breaths.

"I will turn the evidence I have over to the prosecuting attorney so they can unravel the financials, but for now, what I'd most like to find out from you is how did you get the medication Booze asked you for?"

"Excuse me?" Tuttle jerked his head back from his aloof stare.

"The medication," Conrad stated again. "He asked you to find someone he could get Zyprexa from and he did indeed have that in his possession when he died. I'm interested to know who you found to supply him."

"I do not sell drugs, sir." Tuttle straightened his shoulders indignantly. "If that is the focus of your investigation, you are talking to the wrong person. I don't know anything about such things."

"I'm not actually investigating drugs specifically, any more than I'm targeting embezzlement, however both of those things seem to play a role in Mr. Lockhart's death."

"This is absurd. Booze had a heart attack. What's to investigate?" Tuttle threw his hands up in the air and let them fall to his lap. "I have nothing to do with his death. I wasn't anywhere around when that happened, so why am I here?"

"What do you think caused Mr. Lockhart's death?" Conrad leaned forward and turned his head as if he hadn't heard Tuttle's statement clearly. No one had released any public information about Booze Lockhart's cause of death and oddly, none of the people he had interviewed had even asked Conrad about it. As far as he knew, there had been no information leaked.

"Uh, I heard he had a heart attack." Tuttle's voice cracked and Conrad saw beads of sweat pop up on his forehead as Tuttle's face gave away his shattered confidence. "Maybe that was an assumption on someone's part," Tuttle said as he tried to gather his composure. "He lived a rather edgy lifestyle."

"Perhaps," Conrad shrugged. "As to your location however, I think you were quite near when he died, and I suspect Booze was aware of that."

Tuttle's face registered momentary alarm. "Your information must be incorrect."

"I don't think so," Conrad said grinning. "I have a nice picture of you in the alley that night meeting with a friend." Tommy Turner had drawn a startling likeness of Stanford Tuttle standing behind the Old Thyme Italian Restaurant, just three doors away from the Nutmeg Inn. A dark-haired man was sitting in a truck and Tuttle appeared to be in a conversation with him. It might not be useful in court, but it would play well for now.

"Just what are you accusing me of? If you are accusing me of some wrongdoing, this interview is over. I want my attorney present."

Conrad glanced over his shoulder when he heard a tap at the door. "Yeah?"

"Sorry, Chief," Tabor said opening the interview room door a few inches. "He's back. You wanted me to let you know."

"Yes, thanks," Conrad nodded as Tabor shut the door again, and the aroma of pizza wafted into the room. "I apologize but I need to step out for a moment. Before I do though, I want to just lay things out clearly for you and give you time to think."

Tuttle crossed his legs and raised his chin as he struggled to return to his aloof demeanor.

"As I see it, you have a couple of choices at this point. You can continue this charade and I can put you in a holding cell while the State crime lab and the prosecutor's office work out the charges. On the other hand, if you can give me honest answers to my questions so I can continue my investigation, you might be able to return home this evening. It's up to you. Phone a friend if you like. I'll be back in a moment."

Conrad picked up his props and left the room, tossing the folders on the table near the door and saw

Wink with a large slice of pizza in the air just inches away from his open mouth.

"I smell food," Conrad said smiling as Wink fumbled with the large slice.

"I thought you all might be working through dinner," Cora said from the dispatch room. "I was a little hungry myself."

"Well, thank you. Yes, we're always hungry around here," Conrad said. "Grab a slice and join me. I'm going to let Tuttle have a minute to get his ducks in a row in there."

"Did you get my email?" Wink said with his mouth full.

"I did. Tabor found some good stuff on the laptop, too. Tuttle's soaking it all in right now." Conrad grabbed a napkin and plopped a slice of pizza on it.

"I came back to work on that stack of papers you found in the closet. I didn't have time to get through that once I got off the phone," Wink said.

"I'm happy to help if you'd like," Cora said. "I can help sort through it."

"It's right there on that desk," Wink said pointing. "Looks like a mix of business documents and receipts. I glanced at it but didn't see anything about Tuttle."

"Well, this looks like information on land sales to me," Cora said pushing her pizza aside to pull the stack in front of her. "Deeds and mortgages. Maybe this is documentation from Booze selling off his dad's properties."

"I was told he did that, but I haven't had time to research the county property records yet. I think that probably happened a couple of years ago." Conrad took a bite of pizza and chewed quickly. "Georgie? Did you reach the state lab?"

"Yeah, Chief. They still haven't got anything on your prints, but it's still running."

"I got some good prints from the unmarked pill bottle, but all I know so far is they aren't all Booze's prints. I'd hoped they'd find a hit in the criminal database."

"Is Tuttle a certified public accountant?" Cora said. "I think Ohio requires fingerprints to be licensed as a CPA. I know I had to give my fingerprints to the Ohio Department of Education to teach."

"I don't think so," Conrad said. "It wasn't on his business sign."

"I can probably look that up online," Tabor said as he reached for another slice of pizza. "They usually post those things if they issue a business license."

"Check that out for me when you get time," Conrad said scrubbing his hands with a napkin. "I need to get back in there."

Tabor nodded as he continued scrolling through data on Booze's laptop and Conrad grabbed his stack of folders.

"Sorry for the interruption," Conrad said as he re-entered the room with Tuttle. "Now, where were we? Oh yes, I think the ball is in your court. How would you like your evening to end?"

"I'm not trying to be uncooperative, Chief," Tuttle said leaning forward against the table. Clearly, phoning a friend had changed his attitude.

"Glad to hear it," Conrad said sitting in the chair across the table. "Let's revisit the issues. At the time of his death, Booze was angry with you over some changes in his investments. Is that fair to say?"

"Yes."

"Prior, in fact just a day or two prior to his accusations, Booze asked you to secure him some Zyprexa. He told you he needed it and his doctor had failed to provide it."

"He did." Tuttle glanced at the corner of the table again.

"Did you get this medication for Booze?" The friend Tuttle phoned must have advised him to keep his answers brief which was going to require a lot more questions to get to the truth.

"I did not."

"Do you know where those pills came from?" Conrad's impatience was taking over, and he forced Tuttle to meet his eyes.

"I do not."

"So, you took no action at all when you received that email request? Because we have fingerprints running right now at the state lab and if you've ever been fingerprinted for anything in your life, they'll be running them against yours."

Tuttle stared blankly at Conrad.

"What did you do after you got that email? Did you call him, forward the email or talk to someone about it?"

"I don't wish to implicate anyone else," Tuttle said glancing down at his lap.

"Well, you don't have to," Conrad said lifting the folders from his lap and slapping them down on the table between them as he stood. "You're doing a real fine job here of implicating yourself." Snatching the papers back off the table, Conrad turned towards the door. "I've got to make a phone call and make some arrangements for you tonight." Conrad turned the doorknob and glanced back at Tuttle to watch the red hives bloom around his neck. "You know tomorrow being a holiday, might make it harder to reach a judge."

Although Conrad heard Tuttle's meek plea for him to stop, he shut the door and turned the lock anyway. "Guess I went back in too early," Conrad said smiling as Cora, Wink and Georgia all stared at him. "Glad to see you guys at least left me a piece of pizza."

"Is he giving you a hard time, Chief?" Wink asked. "Want me to go in with you?"

"Nah, not really. He's a little guy and he's just having a hard time climbing down off his high horse."

Wink laughed as Conrad heard a radio call from Asher coming into dispatch that they were coming to the office.

"Hide the pizza," Wink said. "Asher will eat it all."

"Did Hudson get anything from the neighborhood canvas?" Conrad asked Georgia.

"Motorcycles, Chief," Georgia said. "Hudson said more than one neighbor saw or heard a bunch of motorcycles around Nellie's place today."

"Those Buckeyes," Wink growled. "Never saw anything good come from a bunch of—"

"They're going to be in our parade tomorrow," Cora said softly.

"You invited them?" Conrad's head jerked around with an angry glare.

"Why, yes. Well, actually Amanda did, but I believe they said they would love to participate."

"Cora, how could you?" Conrad lowered his eyes and shook his head. He never used her given name in front of others, but it slipped out.

Alarmed by Conrad's disappointment, Cora was momentarily speechless. "I thought they would make an interesting addition to the parade. I didn't know they were bad people. Amanda said they were perfectly pleasant when she spoke with them."

"I'd rather not encourage them to come to Spicetown, but I guess I'll know where to find them tomorrow," Conrad said slapping his hand against the side of his leg.

"Yes," Cora said smugly. "And they have to behave while they are in the parade."

"Oh, they'll behave all right," Wink said with a smirk. "Because I'll be walking right along with them."

"Where did you put them?" Conrad asked and saw Cora's hand reach for her handbag.

"They're right behind the scouts and in front of the Sweet & Sour Spice Shop float," Cora said reading from her list. "Ned should be on that float and I thought he could keep an eye on them."

"I'll just walk along with the scouts then and make sure." Wink said as Asher walked into the dispatch room.

"Pizza! Why didn't anyone tell me?" Asher grabbed for a remaining slice and then looked for something to put it on. Grabbing a folded newspaper, he used that as a plate.

"Because we didn't want to see it all disappear," Wink yelled as Georgia laughed.

"The mayor brought the pizzas by for us," Conrad said as Asher shoved half of a large slice into his mouth in one bite.

"Thank you, Mayor," Asher mumbled with a full mouth of food.

Conrad rolled his eyes and reached for the door handle.

"Wait," Cora called out rising from her seat with a paper flapping in her hand. "I did find something."

"What is it?" Conrad walked over and took the stapled long sheets of paper from Cora's hand.

"It's Booze's will. I read over it and it's pretty standard. Almost everything goes to Kathy and his daughter, but he does grant Tuttle a property located in Red River."

"Hmm," Conrad said reaching in his pocket for his reading glasses. "Tabor, can you pull up a picture of where this property is?" Conrad walked over to the desk where Tabor was sitting with Booze's laptop.

"Sure, Chief." Tabor turned and logged into his own computer as Conrad pointed to the property's legal description listed in the deed.

"Right here, Chief," Tabor moved back away from the computer screen and pointed. "At the end of Mulberry Street. The property tax website says there's a house on it."

"Yeah, there is," Conrad nodded and looked at Cora. "That's Tuttle's house."

"Oh, my," Cora muttered.

"But I thought Chief Fairmont told you that was Tuttle's dad's house?" Wink frowned.

"That's what he said. Tabor, look and see who owned it before Booze," Conrad said as he peered over Tabor's shoulder.

"Yeah, it shows a Stanford Tuttle buying it in 1962. Then it shows the county foreclosed for non-payment of taxes."

"That's his dad. Fairmont did say Tuttle was a junior. I bet Booze bought it at auction."

"So how did Booze end up owning Tuttle's house?" Wink continued to frown.

"When you don't pay your property taxes, the county treasurer can initiate foreclosure and then re-sell your house, or they can sell the tax lien. The person buying the tax lien has to wait a year and then foreclose on you to get a deed to your property." Cora tapped a handful of pages against the desktop in an effort to straighten the edges. "The rest of the stuff here is related to Booze's dad. His dad's will and estate papers are here along with details of the bills he paid and property he sold."

"So, Tuttle lived in a house that Booze owned? Wonder if he paid rent to him?" Wink looked at Tabor quizzically.

"I can't get into the financial program," Tabor shrugged. "I haven't figured out the password, but he might have been getting rent payments."

"Or he might have been holding it over his head. Smells like a possible motive," Conrad hummed.

"I also found two insurance policies," Cora said holding the pages up that were bound with a light blue colored backing. "One is payable to Kathy and the other to Stanford Tuttle, Junior."

"Tuttle!" Conrad exclaimed. "Another motive. Let's see what I can find out."

Conrad left the props behind this time and unlocked the door to Tuttle's interview room.

"Well, unfortunately for you, since tomorrow is a holiday, we won't be able to get you before a judge until—"

"This is not necessary, Chief," Tuttle said scooting forward in his chair until his chest bumped against the edge of the table. "I can tell you what you need to know."

"Oh, okay," Conrad said straightening the chair before sitting down and leaning back. "Shoot."

"I don't know where the pills came from—"

"Not the right place to start," Conrad said leaning forward to rise from his chair.

"No, wait. Wait. I mean I don't know who the dealer or whatever was. I only know that I asked this biker if he knew where to get them." Tuttle took a deep breath and leaned back slightly. "I don't know where they came from, but he got them."

"And you gave them to Booze?"

"Yeah, he wanted them."

"And who was this biker?" Conrad was pretty sure he knew the answer to this.

"Just some guy that was a courier for one of Booze's businesses. He brought over the daily receipts and delivered to me."

"Look," Conrad blew out air in frustration. "I already know all about this so just spill the beans. I'm way ahead of you. Holding back isn't looking good on you."

Tuttle was red blotched and sweating, shifting one way and then the other in his chair. "Montana. Montana Black. He's a biker and he ran things for Booze over at Sharpe Auto."

"And he's mad at Booze now, too."

"Well, yeah. He's finally figured out that Booze was cheating him."

"He thinks you're in on it, too," Conrad said raising an eyebrow speculatively. "So, why is he still talking to you?"

"No," Tuttle said quickly. "No, he's not, he doesn't think that. He knows that I'm trying to help him."

"Maybe he's not as stupid as you think either. Looks like you've gotten yourself tied up in a triangle. Looks like you are the one trying to dupe Booze and Montana because you're sitting on the money now. Both of them felt cheated by you and you tried to play one off the other. Let me tell you, you're not any good at it. They were both onto you."

Tuttle slumped back in his chair. "That's not the way it is. I know it looks bad, but really, I was just trying to do the right thing. Make things fair."

"Tell me what you think is fair." Conrad pulled his ankle up over his knee and glared at Tuttle. "Was Booze having ownership of your family home, fair?"

Tuttle glared back with rage in his eyes and Conrad saw he had pushed a button.

"Booze was a jerk. He was cheating everybody and yeah, I think everything he did to me, to Montana, and even to his family, I think it was all unfair."

"So, why do business with him? Why help him cheat everybody?" Conrad shook his head bemused.

"To get my house back," Tuttle yelled. "To get out from under his hold on me."

"So, you were planning to trick him somehow into signing your house over?"

"He was going to use it as collateral for a loan," Tuttle said glancing at the table. "I was going to finance that loan."

"I see," Conrad said letting his foot drop to the floor. "What's in it for Montana? Why is helping you?"

"He has his own interests," Tuttle said quietly. "I could only speculate."

"Well, speculate away!" Conrad shouted. "I don't have all night."

"All right. All right," Tuttle said rattled and panting as if he were hyperventilating. "He had a thing for Booze's wife. I think he thought he could get Kathy if he had money, so he was trying to get more money out of Booze."

"Get more money, how?"

"Doing the same thing Booze did to him. He lied about the hits he made so Booze had to pay him more and he threatened to tell Kathy's attorney about the income Booze was hiding."

"So, the two of you were plotting against Booze for different reasons?"

Tuttle looked down at the table and didn't reply.

"Did you know Booze had a will?" Conrad asked nonchalantly.

Tuttle's head popped up. "You found a will?"

"So, no? You didn't know?" Conrad scrutinized Tuttle's reaction and decided he must not have known about it.

"No, I never knew he had a will. I just assumed everything went to his family. He never mentioned making a will," Tuttle shrugged. "What does it say?"

"I would guess he was about ready to change it, seeing as how he was getting divorced and his friends were betraying him. People usually do after that. He had life insurance, too. Did you know that?"

"No, but I'm not surprised. He loved his daughter despite his problems with Kathy," Tuttle said, relaxing his shoulders.

"He actually had two policies, but neither were payable to his daughter," Conrad waited but Tuttle did not ask. "When was the last time you talked to your brother?"

Tuttle jerked upright at the turn of the questioning. "My brother?"

"Yeah, Randolph Tuttle."

Tuttle widened his eyes in bewilderment. "Years. I don't know. We aren't close. Why would you ask about my brother?"

"Booze did some business with your brother. I thought perhaps you referred him to Randolph."

"Heavens, no. Are you sure? He never mentioned it to me."

"Very sure," Conrad nodded. "In fact, your brother did Booze's will for him. Seems one of them would have mentioned that to you."

"No."

"Especially since you're in it," Conrad said as he leaned back to watch the reaction.

"I'm in Booze's will?"

"Indeed, you are," Conrad said smiling. "Tell you what, I'm going to let you go home tonight and I'm going to do a little more digging around. Make sure I can find you when I need to, okay? No more playing hide and seek. When I call, you better answer. Okay?" Conrad stood and walked to the door.

"But wait, Chief. What's—"

"Have a good holiday, Mr. Tuttle." Conrad opened the door and left it standing wide as he walked out into the dispatch area. Moving his head to signal Cora and Wink to follow, they all walked down the hallway to Conrad's office where he quietly shut the door.

"You're letting him go?" Wink whispered as Cora frowned in confusion.

"Yeah, he didn't mean to kill Booze. He was just trying to cheat him. Funny how it all panned out."

"Huh?" Cora looked lost.

"Tuttle was trying to get Booze in a situation where he needed money enough to put up Tuttle's house for loan collateral. Tuttle was going to finance that loan with the money he'd stolen from Booze. Then when he couldn't repay the loan, Tuttle was going to force Booze to forfeit the house back to him," Conrad laughed. "All that work and all he really had to do was kill Booze to get the insurance money and the house back. He was so busy trying to outsmart Booze and Montana, he was the stupid one."

"What?" Wink paused. "So, he didn't get the pills?"

"Yes and no," Conrad shrugged. "He asked Montana to do it, but it wasn't because he was trying to kill Booze."

"So, Booze's death is an accident?" Cora seemed disappointed.

"I still don't think so, but it's too early to place bets yet. I need to hear back from the lab on the prints and Alice is still waiting on some medical info. The holiday may delay some of that, but I think I'll know soon."

"Speaking of holiday…" Cora put her hand on the doorknob. "I think I'll be heading home now. Big day tomorrow."

"Yes," Conrad said sighing, secretly wishing it were over. "We'll see you bright and early. Right, Wink?"

"Yeah," Wink nodded and then frowned. "I'm shooting for early. I can't promise I'll be bright though."

Cora snickered and pulled open the door. "I'll take what I can get. Have a good night, boys."

Sheri Richey

Chapter 16

Cora dabbed at her face with a powder puff and looked in the mirror. "Oh, it's hot already. I'm a mess." Chaos was all around the school parking lot as the floats and bands lined up. Jimmy Kole was yelling at everyone through a megaphone and Amanda was tugging on Cora's arm as she slipped her compact back into her purse.

"You need to get up there, Mayor. The Spicers are already in the car and the Chief has already started to roll."

"I know. I know," Cora said flapping her hands. "I need somewhere to put my purse."

"I can put it in the truck," Amanda offered.

"That's okay. I'll just stuff it in the floor. You need to get on your float, too."

"Bryan's taking care of it and I'm farther back. You've got to go *now*." Amanda saw that kind encouragement wasn't working and the mayor was about to hold up the whole parade.

Scurrying to the Mustang convertible, Cora climbed into the backseat. Mike was in the seat beside her and Bradley was sitting on the back of the seat between them with his legs dangling. His grandmother, Ellen, was riding in the front. Her ·clerk, Laura, was in the driver's seat. "I see your dad decided to let you drive," Cora said patting Laura on the shoulder.

"Ready, Mayor?" Laura said, smiling in the rear-view mirror.

"I'm ready," Cora said stuffing her purse in the floor. "You're welcome to get on the back if you'd like," Cora said to Mike Spicer. "I just feel better sitting in a seat. We don't want to lose Bradley."

"I'm with you," Mike said. "I'd rather be here, and we'll just grab his legs if he starts to fly out." Bradley laughed as Cora and Mike both grabbed an ankle.

As they pulled out of the school parking lot, Cora heard the rumble of motorcycles and glanced back with a twinge of regret that she had invited the Buckeyes. She saw Wink walking behind the scouts in a polo shirt and jeans appearing to be a part of their group and felt some reassurance he would keep an eye on them. Remembering that Wink had planned to bring his dog, Hank, she looked again, but didn't see Hank anywhere.

As they hit the street and approached the onlookers in their red convertible with a *Grand Marshal & Founder's Family* sign on the side, Cora waved and smiled at the crowd. Bradley was pivoting from side to side, grinning ear to ear, and waving both hands. She wondered if he could keep that up for the whole parade.

"I can't hear you over those bikes," Conrad yelled into his car speaker as he coasted down the street. He had Wink on the phone and Wink could hear fine through the ear buds, but Conrad was picking up all the motorcycle sound from Wink's microphone.

"Okay," Wink said holding the mic close to his mouth. "I can hear you fine though, remember?"

"Sorry." Conrad laughed, realizing he was yelling over noise that Wink didn't hear.

"So, who's with Montana?"

"Three guys," Wink said. "One of them is that fat old bald guy we saw at the shop. I don't know the other two."

"Are they behaving?"

"Yeah, they're doing okay. Circling around a bit and even waving occasionally when they see a pretty girl. I could do without the revving of the motors, but the kids don't seem to mind."

"Okay, stay with them at the end if you can. I'll be at the statue dedication in the park."

"Gotcha," Wink said as he punched the button to end the call but left the ear buds in place.

Conrad turned his siren on again to compete with the fire engine following him and waved at the excited children on the side of the street. Not surprisingly, Sheriff Bell had reneged on his promise to participate when he learned his car would be placed second behind Conrad. Naturally, Bobby Bell told Amanda it was due to a scheduling conflict.

Looking between the buildings as he passed by the Sweet & Sour Spice Shop, he saw four motorcycles parked without their riders. Montana must have brought the whole gang here today somewhere. It seemed odd they would choose a spice shop to be their central meeting point, especially since it had limited access today with the parade going by.

Conrad chuckled because he could hear Cora's voice in his head saying, maybe they just wanted to see the parade, too. Although Cora Mae reduced everyone she saw into the 10-year-old child she remembered, it seemed that parades made her a 10-year-old girl herself and she loved them. He couldn't bear to tell her he would be happy to see them outlawed completely.

Flipping off the siren, Conrad saw an incoming call on his dash monitor. "Yeah, Sammy. Can you hear me?" Sam Crawford was working dispatch today because Georgia had a booth at the Market Days craft fair.

"Yeah, Chief. Sorry to call during the parade, but I just heard from the coroner. She got some results back on your pills and wants you to call when you're free."

"Thanks, Sam."

Conrad checked the time and thought he'd have a chance to call while he waited for the parade to end. Being the first in line had its advantages. He was eager to get those results.

§

As the parade was winding down to an end, Cora glanced up at Bradley. She had expected him to be exhausted from all the greetings he had given, but he was still wearing his smile. "I think I may need to hire you for my next parade, Bradley. I could use someone to wave and smile for me."

Mike Spicer chuckled as Bradley dropped down between them on the seat. "I think he'd probably do it for free."

"Yeah, this was fun," Bradley said pointing at the parking lot. "Nobody's going to get their car out of here. Aren't you glad you didn't drive over, grandpa?"

All the parade participants were filing in the lot along with their vehicles and floats and all the parking area was blocked in.

"That's okay," Cora said. "You can ride with me. I've arranged for Rodney to pick us up."

Cora climbed out of the backseat of the convertible last and stretched. Next year she hoped they found a car that was a little roomier. Fluffing her copper-colored hair with the palm of her hand, she wished for a private moment to fix her face. The heat was melting her makeup off and she pulled a notebook from her large purse to fan herself.

"There's Rodney," Bradley yelled pointing as Rodney drove around the people milling about in a small canopied golf cart. "We get to ride in that? Cool!"

"Oh, my," Cora said with a twinkle in her eye. "Where did you come up with this?"

"Can I ride on the back?" Bradley said jumping on the back seat as his grandparents stepped into the rear seat.

"I'm going to hang onto you," Mike Spicer said sternly as his wife, Ellen, frowned with concern.

"Don't worry," Rodney assured them. "I'll go really slow."

"Where did this come from?" Cora asked again as she slipped into the front seat and put her purse between her ankles so she could hold on.

"My wife, Carmen, is friends with the Buckleys that own that driving range south of town. She asked them if we could borrow it, so they brought it in with them this morning. They're doing something at Market Days."

"Tanner Buckley?" Cora asked over Bradley's squeals of delight.

"Yeah, his wife paints or something. They've got a booth."

"How nice," Cora said. "Well, this is a treat. It rides better than I expected. I'd like to have one to buzz around town in. Think the Chief would let me?"

Rodney's eyes got wider than his smile as they chuckled at that image. "I don't know about that. Better ask him first," Rodney said as he pointed at Conrad who was standing over near the trees talking into his phone with one hand while holding his opposite ear closed with the other hand.

"He can be a real party pooper sometimes," Cora said with a pout.

"I'm going to do security detail later and I thought it'd be great to do it with the golf cart. Then I can cover a lot more territory."

"Yes, that's an excellent idea," Cora said as the cart came to a stop near the podium.

"I'm going to leave it parked over here while I film your speech. I hope nobody bothers it."

"Just tell Bradley to keep an eye on it. I'm sure he'll be happy to have that job." Cora glanced over her shoulder to see if Bradley heard her, but he had already jumped down and was running to the podium chairs.

"Bradley," Ellen yelled and then motioned him back with her hand when his head turned. Bradley jogged back toward them. "You can't run off like that. I can't chase you around. You need to stay close to us today. I'm afraid I'll lose you in the crowd."

"Ah, grandma. I'm not a little kid."

"Bradley," Cora said abruptly to distract him from his angst. "Rodney has an assignment for you."

"Oh, you do? What is it?" Bradley instantly perked up and presented himself for duty.

"I've got to film the mayor's speech so I'm going up there," Rodney said pointing to a second-story window in the building next to City Hall. "I need someone to keep an eye on the golf cart for me."

"Sure," Bradley said standing up straighter. "Can I drive it?"

Rodney chuckled. "No, it doesn't belong to me and I can't loan it out. I'm going to park it right over there by the trees. You'll be able to see it from where you're sitting and just make sure nobody bothers it. Okay?"

"Okay," Bradley nodded. "When we're done, I'll go sit in it until you get down."

"Okay, sounds good." Rodney rubbed Bradley on the head and waved as he pulled the golf cart over to a shady spot near City Hall.

"I wish I'd thought to have someone put up an awning for us. There's no shade by the statue." Cora pulled a tissue from her bag and dabbed at her forehead.

"We can just wait by the golf cart until it's time to start," Ellen suggested as Mike put his arm around her shoulders.

"Good idea, honey. It even gives us somewhere to sit while we wait."

"And nobody can steal it," Bradley added.

"That's right," Cora said with a smile. Waving to Conrad when she caught his eye, she pointed to the golf cart and turned to follow the Spicers to the shade.

§

"Alice, I'm not sure I'm understanding you. Are you saying the pills were tampered with?" Conrad struggled to hear over the din of people approaching the sitting area around the statue. He waved at Cora to let her know that he saw she was going over in the shade to wait for the presentation to start.

"No, it's not that exactly. They aren't standard. A couple of things," Coroner Alice Warner struggled to explain. "The pills don't match each other. It's like they came from different manufacturers or were different strengths. I noticed that just looking at them. They were irregular. So, at first I'm assuming some old were mixed with new maybe or two different sources. Turns out they were different strengths of the same medicine."

"So, he couldn't tell how much he was taking?"

"A risk you take when you buy on the street," Alice said. "He must have been told to take several though because his tox levels were really high. Maybe he asked for twenty milligrams and the supplier told him the pills had five milligrams in them, which some of them did.

He might have been taking them four at a time. The problem with that is a lot of these pills were twenty milligrams and taking four of them—"

"Could give him a heart attack?" Conrad saw the dilemma now.

"It could," Alice said. "Any idea how long ago he got these pills?"

"My guess is at least two months ago. He asked his friend to get him some back in April. He didn't specifically ask for any particular strength though."

"He obviously read something, or someone told him it would correct his Alzheimer's symptoms. People think taking more of something is better or will work faster. It was probably making his symptoms worse, so he took more."

"I don't have the source of the pills confirmed yet, but I do have a lead. I'm just waiting on the crime lab."

"I'll hold my report until Monday. Nobody's working much tomorrow anyway. Let me know what you find out."

"I will. Thanks, Alice."

Conrad glanced around for Wink, but he didn't hear any motorcycles revving, so he assumed Wink was off following the Buckeyes. As many people walked across the street to hit the Market Day offerings early, several milled around the chairs in front of the statue waiting for the event to begin. Conrad crossed the platform and headed to the shade where the golf cart was parked.

"Did you enjoy your parade, Mayor?" Conrad said when Cora turned around and saw him approaching.

"Hey, Chief," Bradley said from his back seat on the golf cart. "I'm watching the golf cart for Rodney, so nobody steals it."

"That's a good thing," Conrad said to Bradley. "It's too hot today to chase after thieves."

"I think everything went really well," Cora said. "At least as far as I know there were no disasters."

"We made it out alive," Conrad teased. "At least I could run the air conditioning in my car."

"Ugh, it is so hot today. I've been melting," Cora fanned herself with her folded speech. "There's Amanda."

"You found some shade," Amanda said as she joined them. "It looks like everyone is settling in. Are you about ready to start?"

"Don't you need to be at your booth?" Cora knew that Amanda was planning to help Bryan with his store's tent.

"Oh, Bryan is there, and I told him I'd be there as soon as the dedication ended. I wanted to warn you, though. I saw Larry Langley hanging out over there on the side. I'm sure he'll be in your audience."

"Probably just to heckle me," Cora said scanning the crowd. "He's already tested my patience enough."

Mike Spicer frowned. "Who is Larry Langley?"

"Oh, he's a councilman and we are a bit at odds right now," Cora said dismissively. "Actually, we pretty much stay that way."

Amanda giggled and shrugged when Ellen seemed alarmed.

"I hope it isn't over the statue," Ellen said.

"Oh, no. He's mad at me because… Well, it's a long story, and it's a pitifully petty story at that. I won't trouble you. I see Rodney is giving me the thumbs up from the window." Cora pointed to the building next door. "I guess I'll get started. Shall we move to the hot seats?"

"Would you like me to introduce you?" Conrad asked as the Spicer family walked toward the chairs behind the podium.

"Thank you, but that's not necessary. You two stay in the shade." Cora walked to the microphone as Amanda sat down in the golf cart and looked for Larry Langley.

Sheri Richey

Chapter 17

"Hello, everyone," Cora said as she adjusted the height of the microphone. "Can everyone hear me okay?" Looking around she saw smiles and heads nodding.

"I know it's a terribly warm time of day for this so I will try not to keep you too long. Let me introduce my guests," Cora turned sideways to look at the Spicers and saw Bradley sitting between his grandparents and waving to the crowd.

"On your left is John Michael Spicer. He is the great-great-grandson of the founder of our beloved Spicetown, John Joseph Spicer. And on your right, is his wife, Ellen." Cora joined in the applause.

"And our special surprise guest, seated between his grandparents, is John Bradley Spicer. Stand up, Bradley. He is the great-great-great-great-grandson of our founder." Bradley waved both hands wildly as the crowd cheered louder. The young man clearly knew how to win over a crowd.

"I'm so happy you could join us today for this special event." The crowd settled and Bradley returned to his seat, so Cora continued.

"I've looked forward to this for a long time. It's been a dream of mine for this town to keep the history alive and remember the man that started it all, John Spicer. Many of you may have heard me talk about John Spicer before, but I think it's important for our future to not forget our past.

"John Spicer found this beautiful piece of undeveloped land and decided he wanted to stay here, just as we all have. Once a mail stop was created, he convinced others to join him and create the beginnings of our town. John Spicer pulled the mail bag as the U.S. Mail began delivery by railway, so they labeled the train stop Spicer Town. In 1881, the town adopted the name Spicetown and officially marked this place on the map for us all to enjoy.

"When the City Council refused to support my vision of erecting a statue to commemorate our founder, my assistant, Amanda Morgan, helped me find a way to bring this to you today by applying for a historical grant." Cora waved her hand out to the side to turn everyone's attention to Amanda, who was still sitting in the golf cart. Amanda wiggled her fingers in a bashful hello.

Cora paused for the audience to applaud.

"I hope you will be happy with our efforts and take a moment to meet our founder's family today as they visit the fair. Without further ado, let me introduce you to John Joseph Spicer." Cora turned and backed away to the side as Jimmy Kole pulled a rope from behind the statue. The white plastic covering slipped off the statue and fell behind it in a heap as Jimmy rushed to pull it out of view.

Cora beamed as everyone stood up clapping and bubbled with excitement when she even heard whistles from the crowd. Staring up at the dignified bronze man, she felt a wave of tears brimming that she had to push back down as they burned her throat.

Paulie from the Spicetown Star was crouching off to the side shooting photographs and she saw several people in the audience holding up their phone. When the crowd relaxed, she returned to the podium.

"Thank you, everyone. Now, please, go enjoy all the wonderful things at the Market Days fair and remember, the fireworks start at nine o'clock tonight. Thank you." Cora switched off the microphone and stepped back to thank the Spicers. The speech she had been fanning herself with was far too long to read in this heat and she knew Amanda was right. She always had to write them, but she rarely ever read them.

§

"That was shorter than I expected," Conrad said to Amanda as he leaned against the cart.

"She wrote a long speech."

"She must have decided it was too hot to keep people out here very long."

"She's using it as a fan instead." Amanda shook her head and Conrad laughed. "At least she didn't hit the

City Council too hard. The speech was much spicier, and Larry Langley is standing out there at the back of the crowd. I was concerned he might act out today."

"Are they into it again?" Conrad saw Larry talking to his wife. "Why is he even here? I thought he didn't want the statue."

"He didn't, but he wanted credit for it once she figured out how to make it happen. He wanted to be on stage with her and she shut that right down."

"I see," Conrad said smiling and secretly wishing he'd been there for that conversation. He didn't care for Larry Langley either.

"You're right, Amanda dear," Cora said as she walked over to the golf cart. "I don't read my speeches. I just write them." Cora said smiling.

"Well, you needed a fan," Conrad said as Amanda nodded.

"Indeed, I did. It's a lovely statue though and I'm very pleased. At least Larry didn't yell obscenities at me."

"The day's not over," Conrad said as Cora saw his eyes dart behind her. Turning around she saw Larry Langley heading her way.

"You don't happen to have the keys to this golf cart, do you?" Cora smiled when Amanda giggled at Cora's sinister plot to run away.

"Hi, Larry," Cora cooed as she stretched out her hand to shake his. "Have you met our guests, the Spicers?" Cora grabbed Larry's elbow and pulled him toward Mike and Ellen, who were visiting with some people that had approached them after the ceremony. "Let me introduce you."

Conrad gave Amanda a sly smile as they listened to Cora butter Larry up with introductions. Once Larry began chatting with Mike Spicer, Cora returned to the shade with Amanda and Conrad.

"You deflected that nicely," Conrad said nodding his head in appreciation.

"Oh, it's just a short diversion. He won't let it go that easily," Cora said, as she turned her back on Larry's chat with the Spicers. "Do you need to get back to Bryan's tent now? Rodney should be downstairs any minute and he'd probably give you a ride there in the cart."

"That's okay," Amanda said. "We're just around the corner on the right. It's not far."

"As much as I'd like to leave Larry here, I feel like I need to check with the Spicers before I wander off. The smell of corn dogs is making me hungry. I want to stop at the food trucks first." Cora glanced over her shoulder and saw Bradley quizzing Larry. She grew momentarily concerned Bradley's frankness might spark Larry's anger, but disregarded that anxiety. Sometimes the truth hurt, and Larry would have to deal with it if that happened.

"Everything went great, Mayor," Rodney said as he strolled up to join the group. "Carmen was up there with me and she's going to run the equipment home for safekeeping. I'll bring it into your office tomorrow."

"Thank you, Rodney," Cora said patting his arm. "You've been such a big help through all this I'm going to put you permanently on my official parade committee."

Rodney blushed as Amanda giggled.

"Thanks. Happy to help. I'm going to start my security detail now, Chief," Rodney said as Amanda hopped from her seat on the golf cart.

"If you see any members of that motorcycle group, the Buckeyes, can you let Wink know? I know he's trying to keep an eye on them, but that might be tough since he's on foot."

"Sure thing, Chief. I'll keep my eyes open. Anyone need a ride before I leave?" Rodney glanced over at the Spicers as they approached the group. Cora was pleased to see that Larry Langley had decided to save his comments for another time and wandered back to his family.

"No, we're fine," Mike Spicer said as Bradley ran up beside him. "We're going to walk around a bit. Thank you for the ride earlier."

"Yeah, thanks. It was awesome," Bradley added.

"Well, enjoy yourself today," Rodney called out as he started the golf cart. "And try to stay cool." Everyone waved as Rodney pulled out.

"Are you hungry?" Cora looked up at Conrad, but he seemed a million miles away. "Are you hungry, Chief?"

"Uh, I could eat," Conrad said patting his protruding stomach. "But I can always eat."

"We're going to walk around a bit first, I think," Mike said. "Bradley's anxious to see everything."

"Okay," Cora said. "I'm sure we'll run into you. You have the phone number with you to call if you need anything, right? If you need a ride back to the inn or just have a question, please don't hesitate to call."

"I've got it," Ellen said patting her purse.

"I need to get to my tent," Amanda said. "Come by and see us today."

"We will, dear," Cora said waving as Amanda ran ahead of the group and around the corner. "Okay, let's go find those corn dogs."

§

"Wink? Where are you?" Conrad said with his cell phone pressed hard against his ear.

"At the Sweet & Sour Spice Shop, out front by the street," Wink said quietly. "They're all inside."

"Why in the Sam Hill do they keep going there? It makes no sense. Who else is in there?"

"Karen Goldman has been in there all day. Ned Carey and Darlene Anderson came back here once the parade ended. They rode on the float. No other customers as far as I know."

"Have you been in there?" Conrad wondered how Wink knew all this from the street.

"When I first got here, I checked in on Karen just to say hi. She was alone, then. I lost them when the parade ended, but I thought they'd come back here so I waited."

"So, are the extra bikes that were out on the side of the building earlier still there? Where are those riders?"

"Don't know, Chief. The bikes are still parked out there. Maybe the ones inside are waiting for them to show up."

"I'm going to call Ned and see if he knows what's going on. I'll call you back," Conrad searched through his phone contacts until he located his friend, Ned Carey.

"Hey, Ned. Can you talk?" Conrad said when Ned Carey answered his phone.

"Sure, just a second..." Conrad heard Ned speak to someone and then the chimes on the door of the store jingled. "I'm at the store and had to step outside. What's up, Connie? I missed you at coffee this morning. You working today?"

"I'm always working, Ned. What's going on at your store?"

"Just got back a short bit ago. I rode on the float this morning and then went to the statue dedication. I saw you up there hiding in the shade. I just walked back from there."

"What's with all the bikers? There were motorcycles parked alongside the shop this morning."

"Yeah, I told them they could park there while the parade was going on. It's just a bunch of guys from that motorcycle repair place in Paxton I told you about."

"So, they're friends now? You planning to run off and join the Buckeyes?"

Ned snorted with laughter. "I don't think they make those leather vests big enough for me."

"Just so you know, Ned. Those guys were in your store the day Booze died and they knew him. I'm assuming that's why they were in there. They're also friendly with Stanford Tuttle."

"Is this a warning, Conrad?" Ned sounded defensive and that had been happening a lot lately. Maybe Ned was too close to this crime.

"Just a friendly heads-up. I wanted you to know what you're dealing with here and protect your reputation. Guilt by association, you know. There's more to this bunch than you may know."

"I appreciate it," Ned said warily before ending the call.

"Wink," Conrad said feeling the slow burn from his phone conversation with Ned. He and Ned had been friends since Conrad moved to Spicetown and he'd never seen this edgy side from him before, not even when he was stressed out over a big legal case. "Any change at the store?"

"Yeah, the others just arrived and went inside. What did Ned have to say?"

"He got his dander all up again. I don't know what's gotten into him lately. He didn't tell me anything, but I tried to warn him off hanging with the bikers."

"Miss Nellie and her brother, Tommy, are coming down the sidewalk right now. Did Hudson get any leads on her break-in?"

"Not to my knowledge. He took a lot of prints and they've been sent off to the lab. The only lead they mentioned is some neighbors heard motorcycles that day."

"Mr. Wink. Mr. Wink." Conrad could hear Nellie yelling and knew from experience she would keep talking to Wink even though he was on the phone.

"I'll let you go. Keep me updated," Conrad said.

Conrad walked back to the retaining wall on the side of the park where Cora was eating her corn dog. He had eaten his in about three bites, but Cora had to put mustard on each bite, so it took much longer.

"Everything okay?" Cora brushed at her lap with a napkin.

"The bikers are all in the spice shop with Ned. I swear there is something up with him. I talked to him the other day and again just now. Both times he's... I don't know, he's just not himself. Gets his back up over every little thing I say. I don't know why he's so defensive, but he acts likes he's guilty of something."

"Well, it still seems odd to me that Booze wanted to buy the place. Of all the places in Spicetown he could pick, why would he single out Ned's little spice shop? There must be a common thread here," Cora said dropping her head in thought. "The other places he pushed his way into were struggling or they were hiding something that Booze threatened to expose."

"Or both," Conrad nodded. "Ned told me that Booze had threatened him with something in his past and I found papers in Booze's luggage at the inn that were stories about an old trial that Ned had."

"Maybe Ned has a secret past," Cora said wistfully. "He's only been city attorney for eight years. Before that he was a trial attorney and spent most of his time in Paxton. I don't remember hearing anything unsavory about him. The City Council must not have had any concerns either when he was hired."

"Well, I read the news articles Booze had. They were about some accusations made primarily against his law clerk at the time. He won a trial back in 1981 and the opposing counsel accused him of getting some evidence illegally. He told the judge that his law clerk gathered that evidence and the judge dismissed the allegations as unfounded.

"Did something happen to the law clerk?"

"The article didn't say. It sounded like the whole thing was over."

"Who was the law clerk?" Cora searched her memory, but she couldn't recall anyone working for Ned here in Spicetown except for legal assistants. Back in 1981, her husband, Bing, had been mayor and he hadn't shared any scandal involving Ned with her.

"The article didn't name them."

"That person might be tied to Booze somehow. Maybe Booze knew something more about that illegal evidence and was trying to use it to get Ned's assets. He seems to look for a weakness and then targets the business. A bit backwards from most investors."

"A lot of time has passed," Conrad said.

"True, but maybe Booze just found out about it."

"I'll have somebody check into it."

"Well, hello Saucy," Cora said laughing. "Did you buy a new hat today?"

Saucy strolled up with his cargo shorts on exposing calves as white as his new Velcro running shoes; a red, white, and blue polo shirt; and a giant sombrero on his head. Conrad had to cover his mouth with his fist when his laughter turned into coughing.

"I did, Mayor," Saucy said smiling. "I didn't have any sunscreen and the drug store is closed today, so I looked for the biggest hat I could find."

"I think you found it," Conrad said clearing his throat.

"Now I'm looking for a towel for my head. This hat is scratchy and it sure is hot today. Are you having a good time?"

"We are," Cora said smiling. "I just finished eating a corn dog. Have you eaten anything?"

"I did. They have these little shish kabobs over there on the side. Little pieces of meat with grilled vegetables. It was quite good."

"Probably better for you than what I had," Cora shrugged.

"Chief, I wanted to ask you about Miss Nellie," Saucy said sitting down on the retaining wall next to Cora and leaning forward to see Conrad. "I heard about the break-in at the Turner house and I was worried about her and Tommy."

"Yes, they're fine. They weren't home when it happened."

"Their door was broken down, but we got that fixed for them," Cora added.

"I went to school with their mother. She was a kind lady. I always worried about her kids making it on their own when she passed."

"I'm sure things are difficult," Cora said. "I think they're doing okay though."

"I see them both around town and they seem happy. Miss Nellie takes my picture all the time." Saucy shook his head. "I don't know why anyone would bother their house."

Conrad smiled remembering the drawings he saw in the house of Saucy. Tommy Turner had an amazing talent. He had captured the quirky look that Saucy had when he smiled and there was no mistaking who it was.

"You know, Chief, things are getting worse," Saucy held up his hands in defense. "I'm not saying it's because of you. Don't misunderstand me. I just mean the world is getting worse and maybe you need more officers to cover things. I know you can't be everywhere."

"Are you looking for a job, Saucy?" Cora teased.

"No, ma'am," Saucy said smiling. "I'm happily retired, but I do try my best to keep my eyes open. It never hurts to be watchful."

"That's true, Saucy," Conrad said smiling. He knew he listened to the police scanner at home night and day. "I'd love to hire more officers, but you'd have to get the City Council to agree to that. They don't seem to think it's a good use of their money."

"Well, they're sure wrong about that. Just like that statue, Mayor. That was a wonderful thing you did for this town and they wouldn't even help you with it. I sure plan to remember all these things when it comes time for me to vote."

"Yes, you should let them know how you feel," Cora said,0 smiling over at Conrad.

"I've tried to talk to my councilman before and he doesn't even want to hear what I have to say. You know I've gone to those meetings before. It doesn't seem to do any good, but I have to say my piece."

"You do try harder than most," Conrad said with a grin.

"I'm sure the Turners will probably be at the fair today. I saw them watching the parade this morning." Cora knew that Nellie had taken a picture of her as she passed.

"I better get back out there. Somebody might be looking for me," Saucy said as he pointed to his armband showing he was on security detail. "See you later."

After Saucy left, Cora turned to Conrad. "I know I should walk around the booths now, but I need some air conditioning. I think I'll just slip in City Hall and rest for a little while before I try to walk the fair."

"That's a good idea," Conrad said. "I'd like to head back to my office for a little while and check on things, too. Everybody should be out and about, so maybe I'll get a little quiet time for once."

Conrad walked Cora back to City Hall and then turned the corner on Paprika Parkway to the police department. Before he could get close enough to see the side door, he heard the roar of motorcycles coming through town.

Chapter 18

"Hello, Miss Nellie. How are you today?" Wink greeted Nellie and Tommy warmly because he had learned that it worked better that way.

"Hi, Mr. Wink. Are you going to the fair?"

"I am here shortly. Did you see the parade today?"

"I saw you walking with the boy scouts. Are you a boy scout?"

"Not anymore, but I was once back in the day," Wink said chuckling and then glanced over his shoulder as he heard the door to the Sweet & Sour Spice Shop open. The bikers began filing out the door and walking to their bikes without paying any attention to Wink or the Turners.

"Oooh, that man's mean," Nellie whispered. "See that man with the red scarf? He tried to steal my camera."

"When did that happen?" Wink saw one of them had a red bandanna on his head, but it was not one of the bikers he had seen before at Sharpe Auto.

"Just yesterday when we were walking home," Nellie said. "He broke it open and threw it. I cried, but Tommy fixed it for me."

"That was a horrible thing to do," Wink said looking at the camera hanging around her neck. "Is it okay now?"

"Yeah, can I take your picture?" Before Wink had a chance to agree, Nellie stepped back and looked at him in the viewfinder.

As the motorcycles all started in unison, Nellie covered her ears and cringed. Tommy was frowning as if the noise was painful. As they sped off down the street, Wink pulled his phone from his pocket. "I need to give the Chief a call. I'll walk with you to the fair, if you like."

"Okay," Nellie said as she and Tommy began walking down the sidewalk.

Following closely behind, Wink dialed the Chief.

"Chief, they're gone on the bikes. I'm walking to the fair with the Turners unless you want me somewhere else."

"No, that's fine. I'm going to slip back to the office for a few minutes. There are some things I want to check into."

"Okay, Miss Nellie told me that one of the bikers tried to steal her camera yesterday when she was walking home. The one she pointed out wasn't one of the guys I remember seeing at the garage, but she knew him when she saw him. She said he broke it open and then threw it on the ground. Sounds like they were looking for film, probably after she'd taken their picture."

"Or after they'd ransacked her house and didn't get what they wanted," Conrad said with a growl. "Give Asher a call and tell him to keep an eye out. He's on patrol."

"Will do," Wink said.

§

"Chief! Perfect timing," Sam Crawford said when Conrad walked in the side door. "I just hung up the phone with the lab. They've got a print match for you on your Lockhart case and they're sending it over."

"Great," Conrad said. "Did they give you a name?"

"Nick Mason," Sam read from the note he'd written. "I've never heard of him."

"Me either," Conrad shrugged. "I won't be here long, but I've got some things to do. Send it to me when it comes in."

"Sure thing, Chief."

Conrad punched the power button on his computer and picked up the phone messages that had been left on his desk. The first one said that Nellie Turner wanted to talk to him. Thinking it must be an old message at first, he frowned when he saw it was just written last night. Pulling out his phone, he called Wink back.

"Wink, are the Turners still with you?"

"Yeah, we're right by the statue. Are you around?"

"No, I'm at the office. I've got a phone message that Nellie was trying to reach me last night. Can you ask her about it?"

"Miss Nellie? Did you need to see the Chief last night? Did you go by the police station?"

"About the pictures? He already knows now." Conrad could hear the conversation clearly.

"No, I mean last night. Did you go back in to see him?" Wink asked again.

"Oh, Oh, wait a minute," Nellie said excitedly. "Tommy, you have it. I found a key."

"You found a key?"

"Yeah, yeah, a big key. Tommy has it. It's in your pocket. No, the other pocket. See, see…"

"Chief, they've got the backdoor key to the Nutmeg Inn," Wink said into the phone.

"Holy Cow! Where did she get it?" Conrad sat down in his desk chair.

"Chief wants to know where you found it, Miss Nellie."

"It was in my yard. Back on the side by my bedroom window. I saw it through the window and went out and got it."

"Did you hear that, Chief?"

"I did. No chance of prints on it now though. If she'll give it to you, we can get it back to the inn. Thanks."

Conrad turned over a dozen scenarios in his mind that could place that key outside Nellie's window, but he didn't have anything solid to back them up.

Shelving that for later, he tossed Nellie's phone message in his trash and logged into his computer.

Opening his email program first, he saw Sam had just forwarded him the criminal history on Nick Mason and he clicked on it to download. Slowly, Montana Black's face appeared. Propping his elbow on his desk and holding his chin in his hand, he studied the list of charges and convictions in his past. Nick Mason was 46 years old and had been in prison twice along with several short stays in various jails around the country. It showed he had spent some time in California and New Mexico in his early days and there were drug charges in his past. The longest prison stay had been in the Montana State Prison, where he did eight years for assault. It must have had some impact on him if he adopted the name.

It wasn't really surprising news. Tuttle had said he had asked Montana to get the pills. All this did was confirm that he did it. Whether he knew the pills had different strengths in the bottle or whether he misled Booze about what he had given him was anyone's guess. He'd have to wait until the prosecutor's office opened tomorrow morning and see if the legal heads thought he had enough to charge him.

Conrad stretched back in his chair and thought about the one loose end he hadn't tied up yet, when another phone message caught his eye. Grabbing it up, he read the note and instantly threw back his head roaring with laughter.

"Working hard, are we?" Cora said as her head popped around the doorway and looked around. "Conrad, why are you in here alone laughing like a hyena?"

"Come on in," Conrad said motioning for Cora to take a seat. "You've got to see this."

"Oh, my," Cora began with just a giggle, but as Conrad continued to laugh, the image overcame her, and she bellowed along with him. "That poor boy."

"Ah, he'll be okay," Conrad said. "It's good for him. He's got to learn just like we all did." The new officer, Adam Reynolds, had written Miriam Landry, the Chamber of Commerce President, a traffic ticket earlier that week and Miriam had left a message she'd received notice of a court date set in Paxton for Monday morning. She was warning Conrad that he better be there to defend this child he had hired because she was going to sue them both. Miriam had a reputation for being ruthless and nasty to most everyone. Adam Reynolds was new in town and he didn't know that yet.

"Is it his first time in court?" Cora's laughter at Miriam's predicament had turned to worry now for young Adam.

"He's gone before, but I don't think anyone showed up. Most of these tickets don't actually come to that."

"You have to at least prepare him, Connie. I mean, she might even spit on him," Cora said as her laughter erupted again. Miriam had spit on her once at a council meeting although she hadn't found it funny at the time.

"I will. I'll talk to him tomorrow and tell him know what to expect."

"I can't even imagine what she'll do," Cora said shaking her head wearily. "I sincerely hope she doesn't win it though or there'll be no stopping her."

"Well, I needed that laugh," Conrad said. "Now let me catch you up on your motorcycle club."

"They're not *my* motorcycle club," Cora said. "I take it you're getting ready to tell me they did something bad."

"Well, the prints came back on the bottle of street drugs that Booze took, and they belong to the leader of the Buckeyes. Tuttle told me that's who he asked to get the drugs for Booze and apparently he did just that."

"Oh," Cora said pensively. Perhaps Conrad had been right.

"The guy has also moved around to different states throughout his life and been in jail or prison in all of them, except Ohio, and I'm fixing to see if I can arrange that for him."

"Well," Cora paused. "I guess that means your case is all resolved now."

"No, not really. I can't prove the guy did anything more than pass illegal drugs. I don't even know if he had any malintent."

"Does he have a motive?" Cora asked. "Is the leader the guy you saw at Kathy's house?"

"Yeah. He told me he thought Booze and Tuttle were both cheating him, but I don't know if I believe him. He's the guy Tuttle keeps having these secret meetings with and Tuttle didn't indicate he had any problem with him. One of them is lying to me."

"Maybe we need to go back to Red River," Cora said. "Once Kathy realizes what you know about the guy, she may be more forthcoming. I felt the whole time we were there that she was playing dumb. She knows more about Booze and his dealings than she lets on."

"I felt the same way, but I had nothing to press her with."

"Well, you do now," Cora said. "Let's go."

§

"We can't go today," Conrad said. "You haven't even walked around the fair and done all that mayor stuff you do. I need to be in town with all the extra people running around."

"This place is quiet as a morgue in here. There's nothing going on. Wink is on duty. He can handle it. I've said my speech and everyone at the fair will just think they must have missed my visit. As long as we're back by the fireworks at nine o'clock, no harm's done. It's only a little after two o'clock now. Let's go!"

"Hang on," Conrad said. "We don't need to drive all the way over there and her not be home. Let me call first."

Cora nodded and sat back in her chair while Conrad looked up Kathy Lockhart's phone number to call.

"Hello. Hello."

"Mrs. Lockhart? This is Chief Harris—"

"Hang on. Shoot. Can you hear me? Hello."

"Mrs. Lockhart? Yes, I can hear you. This is Chief Harris in Spicetown. Is everything okay?"

"Oh," Kathy gasped. "Yes, Chief. Sorry. I'm in Booze's car and I don't know how to work this TV screen thing. When your call popped up, I didn't know how to answer it. I'm sorry."

"That's quite all right," Conrad said smiling. He'd had similar problems when his squad car was upgrade with those options. "I was just calling to see if you were home. I wanted to stop by, but I see you're busy."

"Oh, no, well," Kathy stammered. "Actually, I'm on my way to Spicetown. My daughter, Isabel, spent the night with a friend there and I'm meeting them later for the fireworks. Then I'm bringing her back home with me. What did you need?"

"I had a few more questions, but I don't want to ruin your holiday. We can wait until tomorrow if that's easier and I'll drive out."

"That's not a problem. If you're in the office, I'll just stop by. I was just going to walk around the fair and look around. I'm not meeting the girls until later. Would you like me to come there?"

"Yes, that would be great. Do you know where it is?"

"I do. I'll see you shortly."

"Okay," Conrad said.

"Oh, ah, Chief?"

"Yes?"

"Can you hang up the phone? I don't think I know how to do that yet," Kathy said with a giggle.

"Sure thing," Conrad said, chuckling and clicking the button to disconnect the call.

"So, she's coming here?" Cora deduced from her end of the conversation.

"Yes, she's in the car now, Booze's car. She was coming to town to pick up her daughter. She's going to stop in here first."

"That will be a great time saver," Cora said standing. "Well, I don't think I need to be here when she arrives. I'll walk over to the fair and park myself at Amanda's tent. Text me if you have any updates. I hate to miss all the booths, but with this heat, I don't think I can walk the whole area unless it cools off later this afternoon."

"Okay," Conrad said. "If you decide you need some air conditioning, come on back."

"I will."

"Chief," Sam Crawford called out from the dispatch booth and then jogged down the hallway to Conrad's door. "Check out the parking lot."

Conrad had cameras on the outside of the building that displayed the side door, the front entry door, and a span of the parking lot. The dispatcher had those views on a large screen in his booth and managed the maintenance of a backup tape of all the office outdoor activity. Conrad had a much smaller view in his office on one monitor that sat off to the side of his desk. "They came in like a swarm of bees!"

"What?" Cora turned to frown at Sam and then looked at Conrad.

"It looks like the mayor's motorcycle club is here for a visit," Conrad said as he smiled at Cora with a twinkle in his eye. "A dozen bikes just all pulled into the front lot."

"Oh," Cora said fluttering her eyelashes. "I think I'll scoot right out the side door then. Have fun, boys."

Conrad laughed at Cora's departure and saw Sam's quizzical look. "I tried to tell her not to invite them to the parade, but she thought they were just nice boys on bikes."

Sam nodded.

"You'll probably recognize one of them from the sheet you sent me. Nick Mason is the leader of the group, but he goes by Montana Black. If he comes in, I guess I need to talk to him."

"Okay, let me get back," Sam said as he jogged off down the hallway and heard his radio call out to him. Conrad had hoped to talk to Montana after he saw where Kathy stood on the facts, but if everyone was going to fall right in his lap today, he wasn't going to turn them away.

Sheri Richey

Chapter 19

Conrad watched the TV monitor and saw Montana Black walk away from the group heading to the front door. Relieved that the whole gang wasn't coming inside, Conrad walked out into the lobby to greet him.

"Afternoon, Mr. Mason. What brings you by today?" Conrad didn't detect any surprise register when he used Montana's legal name, but he was dealing with an experienced criminal in Nick Mason.

"Hey, Chief," Montana said extending his hand to shake Conrad's. "I was in town for the parade and wanted to talk to you again, if you've got time."

"I do," Conrad said opening the door to an interview room and ushering Montana in with a wave of his hand. "I've got a lot of new security out at the events today and I can't promise we won't be interrupted, but I've got some time. Have a seat."

Montana pulled out a chair and seemed perfectly comfortable sitting in an interrogation room. He was oozing with self-confidence, so Conrad expected he had cooked up a good story to tell him.

"Chief, I think I'm getting a bad rap," Montana said as he leaned forward with both elbows on the table peering over at Conrad sitting across from him.

"How so?"

"That jerk, Tuttle, is trying to pin something on me and I didn't do anything."

Conrad sat back in his chair with a skeptical scowl on his face. "And what's he trying to pin on you?"

"I know he told you I got Booze some pills, but all I did was carry them to him. I didn't buy them or anything. Mel just told me to take them to Tuttle."

"Mel Sharpe?"

"Yeah, the guy that owns the garage with Booze. Tuttle asked me to get them and I told him I didn't know anybody that did that kind of thing. A week later, Mel handed me a bottle and told me to take them to Tuttle. I just thought Tuttle must have asked Mel for them, too."

"So, you're just the innocent courier who got their prints on the bottle?"

Montana did register momentary surprise at that discovery, but then shrugged. "Yeah, I guess my prints would be there. I picked them up off the counter and put them in a bag before I ran them over to Tuttle."

"You didn't ask Mel about it? Didn't ask him what was in the bottle?"

"No," Montana snapped. "It's not my business what they do."

"But from Stanford Tuttle's perspective, he asked you for the pills and a week later you delivered them.

How is that pinning something on you? It sounds like that is what happened."

"But I told him no and I didn't get those pills. I didn't buy them."

"Illegal distribution of controlled prescription drugs is still a felony and with your sheet—"

"Hey, wait," Montana said falling back in his chair and flinging his arms out to the side. "I'm the victim here. Tuttle set all this up and me, too."

"Okay, so help me understand something," Conrad said as Montana leaned back toward the table and calmed his outrage. "Why are you and Tuttle head to head all the time? You keep meeting him here in Spicetown. I've got pictures of you in the parking lot of the Old Thyme Italian Restaurant. Both of you are driving all the way over here to meet and that's after the pills were already delivered to Booze."

"That's got nothing to do with the pills. I gave him those months ago."

"Okay," Conrad said taking a deep breath. "Just what has it got to do with?"

"I got other business with Tuttle. He never comes in the office anymore, so I make him meet me here. It's a halfway point for both of us."

"Not good enough," Conrad said as he heard a knock on the door. "You think on that answer. I've got to go see what they need out there. I'll be right back."

Conrad walked out of the interview room and saw Kathy standing in the lobby. Sam was talking on the phone and pointed at Kathy to indicate the reason for his knock.

"Mrs. Lockhart," Conrad said motioning for her to approach. "I appreciate you stopping in for me. We can talk in here." Conrad led her to the next interview room and as they passed by the window of the interview room containing Montana Black, he saw her body recoil in shock. "Oh, don't worry. He can't see you. It's a one-way glass. Please, have a seat."

Kathy pulled out a chair nervously and Conrad puzzled at the change in her demeanor. "Can I get you something to drink? Coffee or water? I'm afraid that's about all we have around here." Conrad smiled warmly and tried to put her at ease, but tension was snapping in the air like a bug zapper.

"Oh, no thank you," Kathy said timidly. "Is he in there because of Booze?" Kathy pointed to the room next door.

"You know Mr. Mason?"

"I know he worked for Booze," Kathy said with wide innocent eyes.

"Do you have a couple of minutes? I need to finish this up and I'll be right back."

"Oh sure, Chief. Go ahead. I'm fine here. I have lots of time. There's no hurry." Kathy sat back in her chair and relaxed at the delay.

"I'll be back shortly. Thanks."

As Conrad slipped out of the interview room door, he saw Cora bustle in the side door. "Oh, Connie," Cora said waving her hand in front of her face. "I can't take it. Can I sit in your office for a few minutes? I need some air conditioning and some water. It's just too hot even in the shade."

"Sure, you can. There's water in the refrigerator in there."

"What's going on? I see all the guys are sitting outside on their bikes."

"Yeah, Montana's in one interview room and Kathy's in the other. You can go in and talk to her if you want. I'm not finished with Montana and Kathy's just waiting on me."

"Oh, I could do that," Cora said perking up. "I'll grab some water and go visit." Cora smiled mischievously and Conrad suspected she returned in part because her curiosity was overwhelming her.

§

"Sammy," Conrad said as he approached the dispatch office. "Can you call Stanford Tuttle for me when you get a chance? Ask him if he'd be willing to come to the office. I've got a few more questions for him and I know he doesn't like to be escorted over here in a squad car. I can't really spare anyone today anyway."

"Sure, Chief."

"Oh, and the mayor is going to step in and visit with Mrs. Lockhart while I finish up with Mr. Mason."

Sam gave Conrad a nod of acknowledgment as he answered the ringing phone at his side.

"Sorry for the interruption," Conrad said as he re-entered the interview room with Montana. "I've suddenly had another unexpected visitor. So, where were we? Oh yes, your other business with Tuttle. What might that be?"

"It's complicated, Chief, and it doesn't have anything to do with the pills."

"Humor me," Conrad barked impatiently as the two stared intently at each other in silence.

"Tuttle told me that Booze was threatening him, accusing him of stealing from him. He wanted protection."

"He wanted you to protect him from Booze?"

"From the club," Montana said. "He told me that Booze had been cheating us out of money and he wanted to make it right. He wanted to give us our share, but he needed us to be behind him if Booze got out of hand."

"So, Booze shorts your pay. Then Tuttle shorts Booze's accounts to pad his own pockets. When he gets caught, he gives you a share to protect him. Have I got that right?"

"Yeah, I guess."

"You're right. It does sound complicated, but I guess you all felt Booze had it coming?"

"Yeah, if he'd just been square with us—"

"And how does Kathy Lockhart fit into all this?" Conrad saw a spark of surprise that Montana swallowed quickly.

"She doesn't. I mean Booze cheated her, too, but she didn't have anything to do with any of this."

"No?" Conrad raised his eyebrows in surprise.

"Nah, she's a victim of Booze and Tuttle, too."

"Hmm," Conrad said. "I think part of the trouble here is no one seems to know who is on their team. Tell me about your relationship with Kathy Lockhart."

"I told you. She's going to take over the shop and treat us fairly."

"So, when did you contact her about the business situation?"

"After I heard about Booze," Montana said relaxing back in his chair.

"So, you hear Booze Lockhart is dead and you pick up the phone to call his wife to see what she's going to do with his business interests? That seems a little abrupt."

"No, I called to, you know, give her my condolences. We just got to talking."

"So, you already knew Kathy? You two were acquainted?" Conrad smirked. He suspected they were more than strangers and he didn't want Montana wasting his time telling him otherwise.

"We've been out a few times," Montana confessed and dropped his head. "She and Booze ain't been together for years."

"Did Booze know you were dating his wife?"

"I don't know," Montana said lifting his shoulders in an exaggerated shrug. "He wouldn't care."

Conrad doubted that but nodded. "I thought maybe that's why your relationship with Booze changed. He may not like paying his wife's boyfriend." Conrad thought he saw a light go off over Montana's head and he wanted to thump him on the forehead. Instead, he just raised his eyebrows in question. Obviously, Montana wasn't sophisticated enough to play all these multiple people against one another successfully. He didn't understand human nature.

"Ya think? Maybe. I hadn't thought about that, but you might be right. He never said anything to me about it," Montana said with a thoughtful frown.

"Anyway, where do you and Tuttle stand right now?"

"Nowhere," Montana said with a puzzled expression. "Booze is dead and he's the only reason we talked."

"You've met with him since Booze died."

"Yeah, but just to get the money he still owed us. Now, we're done. Tying up loose ends, you know."

"And you're moving in to the Red River Ranch, waiting for the will to be read?" Conrad was purely guessing but Montana was more gullible than he had expected.

"I guess. Tuttle told me there was a will and we had to wait on that. He's got all of Booze's money right now."

"So, if Kathy doesn't get anything from the will, you'll be gone?"

Montana laughed and gave him a sheepish shrug in response.

"That's what I thought," Conrad said, rapping his knuckles twice on the table. "Sit tight. I'll be right back."

Conrad knocked softly before entering the room where Cora Mae sat chatting with Kathy. As he had expected, Kathy was smiling and relaxed.

"Oh, Chief!" Cora said abruptly turning around. "I was just telling Kathy all about the parade this morning. It's such a shame she had to miss it."

"Our mayor does love a parade," Conrad said chuckling.

"Oh, I do," Cora confirmed.

"Come on back in the kitchen, Mayor, and let me get you some water. I know you were about to have heat stroke when you came in. I'll grab you some, too, Mrs. Lockhart. I'll be right back."

"It was fun chatting," Cora said as she stood up smiling. "But I could use a drink. Enjoy the fireworks tonight with the girls."

"I'm sure we will," Kathy said smiling as Conrad pulled Cora into the hall.

"So, what did she say?" Conrad said as he followed Cora to the kitchen and watched her reach in for a bottle of water.

"She's struggling right now. She doesn't have any money and Tuttle is holding everything until the reading of the will next Thursday. Her attorney has been trying to force them to file a copy so he can see what's in it and she says they'll sue the estate if she isn't reasonably gifted with his assets."

"What does she consider reasonable?" Conrad frowned as he waited for Cora to guzzle some water from the bottle.

"She knows all about Linda Lavender and Tuttle told her that Linda's getting his assets because they had planned to marry as soon as the judge signed the divorce. Kathy's worried that he might have done just that."

"I guess it could have happened," Conrad said. "Maybe we found the old will, but his attorney wasn't helpful when we contacted him."

"That would be an ugly court battle, but I can't imagine that Kathy would come out with nothing. I'm sure the judge would make sure Isabel was provided for, especially with Booze not paying child support like he should have."

"Did you tell her that?"

"I did." Cora raised her chin in the air. "It was a bonding moment."

Conrad chuckled at Cora's clever manipulation tactics. "So, what else did you get?"

"That biker is living with her. He thinks Booze is rich and he wants her money. She said Booze doesn't really have that much money. Most of it was stolen by Tuttle and the other was squandered away. She plans to take what little he had and hope it gets her through school. She's going to enroll in college online next month and plans to have her degree by the time Isabel graduates high school. Maybe then she can afford to send Isabel to college, and they'll make it on their own together."

"Let me guess," Conrad said smiling. "Is she majoring in accounting?"

Cora laughed and shook her head. "She didn't say, but that's a good guess."

"Well, this shouldn't take long."

"Wait," Cora said pulling the refrigerator open and thrusting a bottle of water in his hands for Kathy.

"Oh, yeah. I forgot," Conrad said as he walked back to Kathy's interview room.

Chapter 20

"Mrs. Lockhart," Conrad said as he entered the room and offered her the bottle of water "I'm so sorry. I call you in here and then I get pulled in other directions. I'm sorry for your wait."

"Oh, no," Kathy said with a wave of her hand. "It's no trouble and please, call me Kathy."

"Okay, Kathy, I really wanted to give you an update on things since you're the next of kin and ask a few follow-up questions."

"Okay," Kathy said as she opened the bottle.

"We've had some additional information from the coroner, and it seems that Booze may have had a heart attack that was caused by some medication he was taking. It appears from what I've gathered that he was trying to treat himself medically and without oversight he used improper dosage amounts."

"It was an overdose?"

"Not technically, but the medication is something that really wasn't appropriate for his current health. He'd asked a doctor for it and the doctor had declined so he apparently found another source for it."

"The guy next door," Kathy said pointing her thumb over her shoulder. "He told me Booze asked for some pills."

"Mr. Mason."

"No, his name is Montana Black," Kathy said.

"That's another reason I wanted to talk to you." Conrad leaned forward in his chair. "His real name is Nick Mason and he has a prison record. I saw him at the ranch that day we talked, and I know you have a young daughter. I thought you needed to know."

"I didn't know that," Kathy said quietly with worry etched across her face. "He's moved in with us now. I don't know how…"

"I'm sorry I couldn't warn you earlier. I just got his rap sheet today."

"Well, this could get sticky," Kathy said trying to chuckle light-heartedly, even though Conrad could still see she was troubled by the information.

"What I wanted to ask you about is the woman that came out to the ranch that day. Linda Lavender. What can you tell me about her?"

"Her real name is Sneedman and she's from Red River. She's a lot younger than Booze so I don't think he knew her from Red River. She works at the Wasabi and Booze probably met her there. They've been dating for a while."

"She's told me she and Booze planned to marry once your divorce was final."

"I heard that, too, but not from Booze. He never mentioned her. Stanford Tuttle told me."

"Tuttle knows Linda?"

"Oh, sure. Linda went everywhere with Booze so I'm sure Tuttle knew her, too."

"Have you ever talked to her? I mean, other than the brief meeting at the door when she came by the ranch," Conrad asked.

"Not until after Booze died. I've talked to her plenty since then and I hope I never see her again."

"Has she been bothering you?"

"She had the keys to Booze's car. The car was in the garage and she tried to steal it. I had to call Fairmont and you know I don't like him at all, but he came out and dealt with her. She was just going to drive it away."

"How did you get the keys back? Did Chief Fairmont give them to you?"

"He told her I had possession of the car and it was property assumed to be mine until he was notified otherwise," Kathy said with a curt nod. "She told him she was getting everything in the will, but he told her she had to wait until that happened. That's why today was the first day I could drive it."

"Sounds like he did the right thing," Conrad said. "What kind of car is it?" Conrad remembered Linda driving a white Lexus the day she visited the ranch for her clothing, and he had later found out it was registered to Booze.

"Yeah, I guess. It's a black Mercedes," Kathy said pointing toward the parking lot. "I still think Fairmont is hoping Linda wins and he gets to come back out and take it all away from me."

"I'm sure he's just wanting to keep the peace." Conrad wasn't entirely sure of that, but he hoped it was the case.

"How does Montana Black know Linda? I saw her wave at him the day she came to the ranch to pick up her things."

"I don't know, probably from Booze. Like I said, she was always with him from what I heard. It could have been from Stanford, too. I think she's related somehow to him."

"Oh, really? I didn't know that."

"It's distant, I think Booze said. Something about Stanford's mom was a sister to Linda's grandmother? I may have that wrong, but they're related some way."

"Well, I guess that's all I need right now, and I hope I haven't ruined your holiday too much."

"Not at all. I'm going to head over to the fair for a while. Is it okay if I leave my car parked here? Will it be in the way?"

"No, that's fine. The street parking is probably about full. We'll keep an eye on it for you."

"Thanks, Chief."

Conrad said goodbye and went into the dispatch booth to watch Kathy on the camera outside. She did greet the bikers politely and it was clear she was familiar with them, but she didn't stop and chat. They didn't seem alarmed by her presence either, so Conrad returned to Montana.

§

"Sorry," Conrad murmured as he slipped into the interview room where Montana was getting restless.

"Just one last thing I wanted to ask before you go. How do you know Linda Lavender? I mean, where did you first meet her?"

Montana straightened up in his seat. "She was Booze's girlfriend. I don't know. I met her a while back."

"I saw her wave to you when she came out to the ranch to pick up her stuff. I thought she was a friend of yours. Was she with Booze when you first met her?"

Montana stared down at an imaginary spot on the table and thought for several seconds. "No, I don't think so. Seems like... No, I met her for the first time at Tuttle's office. I remember now because at first, I thought she was dating Tuttle and boy, I couldn't see that happening. I mean, that's a weird couple. Tuttle's all up tight and nerdy and Linda has purple hair."

"So, then Tuttle told you?"

"Nah, Mel told me. I saw her in the shop one day and Mel told me she was with Booze."

"Oh, so Mel knew her?"

"Seemed to," Montana said. "I saw her later with Booze and dancing at the Wasabi. She works out there."

"Did she know about the pills that Booze wanted?"

"Oh, yeah. She was standing right there at the counter when Mel told me to run them over to Tuttle."

"Didn't that seem odd to you? I mean, why couldn't Linda just take them to Booze? Why run them to Tuttle?"

"I didn't think about it. Tuttle asked for them. I can't remember. Maybe I didn't know Linda was dating Booze then. That was two, three months ago or something."

"Okay, thanks. Good chat. Try to be available if I need you again." Conrad stood and pointed a finger at Montana.

"No problem," Montana said as he jumped up from the chair. "I'm clean, Chief. I did a lot of crazy things when I was young, but that's all behind me. That's why I came in here on my own today. I want you to know people are trying to pin things on me because, maybe it's easy to think I'd do it, but I'm clean."

Conrad nodded as Montana left the room and crossed the lobby. Walking over to dispatch, he watched as Montana jogged out to his bike where the gang sat waiting. Montana was guilty of transporting illegal drugs and definitely was being an opportunist by trying to stake out a claim on Kathy, but otherwise, maybe this time, he was basically clean. He could never admit it to Cora, though. She'd never let him hear the end of it.

"Everything okay, Chief?" Sam Crawford asked as Conrad smiled at the monitor.

"Yeah, I need to make a call or two before I leave."

"Tuttle didn't answer when I tried to call him for you and the mayor's in your office," Sam said as the phone rang.

"Okay, thanks."

§

"All wrapped up?" Cora said as she sat in the visitor's chair in Conrad's office with her feet propped up on a box of files he had in the floor.

"Not exactly," Conrad said plopping down in his office chair. "Very close, though."

"You didn't arrest anybody."

"Nope, but I think I'm going to once the sun goes down."

"After the fireworks, I hope." Cora pulled her feet off the box and sat up straight.

"Yeah, it can wait at least that long."

"Well, let's go back to the fair and act like we've been there all day. You can tell me everything while we walk."

Conrad nodded and rose from his chair. He had planned to call Mel Sharpe and find out who asked him to pick up those pills, but that would just take him down a rabbit hole to where the pills came from and right now, he didn't need to chase that lead.

"Sam, I'm headed back to the fair," Conrad yelled down the hallway at Sam Crawford. Cora pushed open the side door as Sam waved to Conrad.

"Wow, it is hot out here," Conrad said pulling his shirt away from his chest as the humidity felt clingy. "It takes a minute to adjust."

"Trust me," Cora said. "You can't adjust to this."

"Maybe you should move these parades to spring and fall."

"I can't move holidays, Connie. I can do a lot of things, but that's out of my control."

"Aw, just make your own holiday. From now on, can't you just say Spicetown was created on April 8th and make that our official town holiday?"

"Actually, I thought about that, making a Founder's Day holiday for the town. Unfortunately, the official naming of the town took place in February of 1881, so I nixed that idea."

"Oh, yeah. No parades in February."

"Agreed," Cora said with a firm nod. "So, is the biker in the clear now?"

"Well," Conrad grimaced. "He's in a gray area. He's got his hands a little dirty, but frankly, he's in over his head. I was expecting a seasoned criminal with some cunning, but what we have here is a simple guy that thinks a little more of himself than he should. It looks to me like he's getting used more than he's getting out of it. He may have done all that previous prison time just because he isn't smart enough to not get caught."

"I'm sure he wouldn't be the first."

"That's true," Conrad agreed. He had met many criminals he felt a little sorry for because they weren't smart enough to keep from being caught and didn't know right from wrong to start with. "He was trying though. He thought he had duped Tuttle, Booze, Kathy and his boss, Mel. I think they all were just using him. That's why he came to me."

"You didn't ask him to come in?"

"Nope, he just drove up on his own. He was worried that Tuttle was trying to put blame on him, and he wanted me to know he's clean."

"But he's not completely. His prints are on the bottle," Cora said shaking her head in confusion.

"For him, that's clean. He thinks just because he transported illegal drugs, he's a victim. He didn't buy them or sell them. It's still illegal, but a decent defense attorney could easily show he didn't know what he was transporting, and he was complying with a demand from his superior. He'd probably get the charges dropped."

"So, he walks in your door and admits to breaking the law, so you'd know he was clean?"

"Yep. I told you, he's not cunning, but I don't think he was involved in any plot to kill Booze."

"Kathy seems to have the most motive," Cora said pensively. "Once the divorce was final, she might never see a penny from him. A court order for money or assets doesn't mean they actual hand it over. He could just tie her up in court for years and Isabel would be grown before it ended."

"Very true," Conrad said. "But you need motive and opportunity."

"Chief! Mayor!" Harvey Salzman waved a hand in the air as he walked out of the entrance to the fair.

"Hey, Saucy. Are you headed home?" Conrad saw sweat running down Saucy's face, but the towel on his head under the sombrero made his cheery smile contagious.

"Yeah, Chief. My shift is over. I've walked every corner of that fair and tried every food there is to eat. I think it's about time for a nap now."

"Oh, Saucy. I don't know how you did it with all this heat. You must be exhausted," Cora said. "I hope you've been drinking a lot of water."

"Oh, yeah. I've had water, lemonade, slushes, snow cones, you name it. I couldn't say no to anyone." Saucy threw his arms open wide and beamed as if it was the best day of his life.

"You look like you had a good time," Conrad said.

"The best!" Saucy rocked up on his toes and back again.

"I'm so pleased," Cora said as she squeezed Saucy's sweaty arm.

"Was there any trouble out there today?" Conrad hadn't heard anything from Sammy, so he had to assume Wink handled any problems that arose.

"Naw. I ran off a few meddlesome kids at one booth and cleaned up a knee when a little girl fell down. Other than that, I didn't see anything except happy people. It was a great day."

"Well, you go home and rest now. The Chief and I are going to make the loop around and check on things before the booths start closing up. You've had a long day and you've done a great service to your community, Saucy. I want you to know we both really appreciate your security volunteer effort today."

"Oh, I loved it," Saucy said clasping his hands together. "I'm already planning for next year. I'm going to get myself one of those little battery-operated fans you can carry and a belt holster to put my water bottle in. I'll be ready next year, all prepared."

Cora threw back her head in laughter. "Looks like you've got a fourth of July regular now, Chief."

"Looks like it," Conrad said chuckling. "Welcome aboard, Saucy. Maybe we'll have tee shirts printed next year and get you a proper hat."

"Gee, that'd be great, Chief. See you guys, later," Saucy said waving as he trotted down the sidewalk.

"Cora Mae," Conrad said glancing sideways at Cora. "You've created a monster."

"A sombrero wearing monster," Cora muttered as they both laughed their way into the fair.

Chapter 21

"So, what did you think?" Cora asked Conrad as she stretched out her legs before standing.

"They were loud enough."

"They were beautiful," Cora said standing up from her lawn chair where she and Conrad had watched the fireworks display. "I don't know where Rodney went. I need to get his lawn chairs back to him."

"I think he went up there with Wink to keep an eye on the display. We wouldn't want a repeat of New Year's Eve happening," Conrad said with a quiet smile.

"We sure don't," Cora exclaimed. "Well, overall I've been really pleased with the events today. It was too hot for my comfort, but I think everyone had a good day. I've got to talk with Paulie from the Spicetown Star and then my day is done. I may even take tomorrow off work and rest. I guess you've still got work to do."

"Yeah, but I'm hoping it doesn't take too long. If it doesn't go well, I'll just lock everybody up and come back tomorrow to finish."

Cora laughed. "I think you actually mean that."

"I do," Conrad said. "A lot more than you mean to take tomorrow off. I know better. You'll be there just like always."

"You're probably right."

"Here, Mayor. Let me take that," Rodney said as he walked up and took the folded lawn chair from Cora's hand. "Carmen has the van right over on the side and I'll just run them over there. Do you need a ride home or anything?"

"You can ride with me and the Chief, Mayor," Wink said as he strolled up. "I'm going out on patrol anyway."

"Thank you, Rodney, but I'll go with Wink. You've been a big help to me today and I appreciate everything you've done."

"Not a problem, Mayor. It was a fun day. I'm going to take the Spicers back to the inn now."

"Oh, I hope they had a nice time," Cora said, wishing she had spent more time with them. "Be sure and tell them we'd love for them to visit us again real soon."

"I think they've had fun. Bradley's worn them out with all his energy, but I know he had a good day. I took some pictures of them with the statue this afternoon and I think Bradley's parents are planning a trip to see it for themselves. They just couldn't come for this event."

"Well, good. I'm glad to hear that," Cora said as Rodney waved goodbye. "Wink, I'm ready whenever you are."

"I'm ready," Wink said. "My car's right there on the side."

§

After dropping Cora Mae off at her house, Conrad moved to the front seat of Wink's squad car. "Who do you have on patrol right now?"

"Asher and Reynolds are out."

"I'm going to call Asher. I need him to run an errand for me." Conrad pulled out his cell phone to dial and Officer Asher answered.

"Asher, I need you to run out to the Wasabi and pick up an employee out there called Linda Lavender. Do you know her?"

"Purple hair?"

"Yeah, that's her. She should be working, and I need to talk to her. Tell her I found Booze's will and I need to see her. She won't give you any trouble."

"Sure thing, Chief." Asher said and Conrad disconnected the call.

"Asher will love that. He's always wanting to go inside the Wasabi," Wink said grinning.

"I don't want to drive to Red River again. I'm going to check and see if the Red River Police will help me out, but if they won't I may need to send Asher over there to get Tuttle. He didn't answer his phone today when Sam tried to call him."

"That shouldn't be a problem. I don't expect any trouble tonight. We had a good turnout, and everybody should be too tired to cause problems. We'll have some firework complaints, but hopefully that's all."

"I don't want to be out of town, since you are off duty tonight." Conrad slept better knowing Wink was covering night shift, but he had switched to days this week for the parade.

"I thought I'd stick around until after midnight. You're going to be tied up for a few hours and I'm not feeling confident about Reynolds and Asher together yet."

"I understand," Conrad said. "But I think Reynolds is going to be fine with some experience under his belt."

Wink nodded as Conrad picked up his cell phone again to search for the number of the Red River PD.

"Red River PD, Officer Williams speaking. How can I help you?"

"Evening Officer. This is Chief Harris over in Spicetown. I know it's probably too late for Chief Fairmont to be in, but—"

"The Chief is here if you'd like to speak to him."

"Yeah, that would be great. Thanks."

"Connie! You're working late tonight," Dan Fairmont chuckled. "What's up?"

"You're working pretty late, too. Holidays are grand, aren't they?"

"Sure are," Fairmont groaned with sarcasm.

"Well, I'm needing Stanford Tuttle and he's not answering his phone for me. I talked with him earlier and I thought I'd made it clear he needed to keep himself available to me, but maybe that's slipped his mind. Now, I know he doesn't much care for riding in a squad car, so I was hoping you had an officer free to go knock on his door."

"I'm sure I can rustle one up. You want him to come tonight?"

"I do and if I don't hear he's on his way in the next thirty minutes, I'm going to send somebody over for him. He won't have the option of driving his own car this time."

"Sounds urgent," Fairmont said, and Conrad felt the unspoken tug from Dan Fairmont to share his need for Tuttle, but Conrad still wasn't feeling secure about Dan's involvement with Tuttle or Booze.

"It's been a long day and I'm not in the mood to chase people right now. I'm sure you know how that is."

"Sure do, Connie. I'll send somebody over there and try to get Tuttle on the road to you."

"Appreciate it," Conrad said as he disconnected the call.

"You think he'll come?" Wink asked as he pulled the squad car into a parking space near the side door.

"Yeah, I think so." Conrad smiled. "I think he's afraid to ride with Asher."

Conrad turned on his desk lamp and pulled out a pad of paper. It was time for a Cora Mae list. He had some loose ends to tie up with Tuttle and some angles he needed to explore with Linda. He wanted to wrap things up tonight.

The list for Linda was short, but much depended on the way she reacted. She hadn't impressed Conrad as much of a thinker either, but sometimes that was an act.

Tuttle was definitely the smarter player in this triangular game, but he couldn't control his emotional responses well and body language failed him. He had the recorder set up in interview room two just for Tuttle. That added attention might just push him over the edge.

"Chief," Asher said strolling into Conrad's office. "Miss Lavender is here." Bending forward, he thrust out his chest and tossed his head left and right imitating Linda's swish of her ponytail. Conrad chuckled as Roy Asher fluttered his eyelashes. "She's really laying it on thick tonight, Chief."

"Did she try to sweet talk you?"

"Heavy syrup," Asher said, tugging his waistband up over his bulging stomach. "You know that nonsense doesn't work on me."

"I know you're tougher than that, Roy," Conrad said to stroke Asher's flaming ego. "Thanks."

"Anytime. She's in interview room one."

Conrad gathered his file and walked down toward the dispatch booth where Georgia Marks had relieved Sam Crawford. "Georgie, I'm going in room one, but if Stanford Tuttle shows up, put him in room two for me."

"Okay, Chief. He's on his way. The Red River PD called and said Tuttle was driving in."

"Good. Thanks." Conrad opened the door to interview room one.

"Evening, Miss Lavender. I'm Chief Harris. We met a few days ago." Conrad pulled out a chair and put his ankle over his knee to create a table for his file folder.

"I remember, Chief. You can call me Linda. Lavender isn't my real name, you know." Linda batted her long fake eyelashes with tiny rhinestones glued to the edge of her eyelids.

"I'm sorry we had to pull you out of work but with the holiday, it's been a busy day." Conrad found it difficult to look at Linda's overly painted face without being distracted by all the glitter.

"That's okay, Chief. We really didn't have much business tonight. I thought it would be packed since it's a holiday. Maybe tomorrow night will be better. The weekends are usually busy."

"When we first talked a few days ago, I asked you about medication that Booze took. Can you tell me why he was taking medication?"

"I don't know. He said he needed it. It's not like he was taking illegal drugs or anything. He had a doctor and stuff," Linda said.

"Recently, I've learned a lot more about Booze and that's made me wonder about some things. Now, how do you know Mel Sharpe?"

Linda sat back some and straightened her shoulders to adjust to the topic change. The blankness in her eyes confirmed Conrad's first impression that she wasn't a fast thinker.

"He's from Red River. I grew up there, so I've known him my whole life, I guess."

"He's a bit older than you are, I suspect."

"Oh, yeah. His son was a year behind me in school. I don't know exactly when I met him. I've just always known him."

"Yet, you didn't always know Booze? He's from Red River, too."

"Yeah, but he didn't live there when I did. He moved away and when he came back, I was gone. I knew about his family. I mean, I knew his dad lived out there on Red River Ranch when I was a kid, but I didn't actually know his dad or anything. His dad owned a bunch of stuff in Red River."

"Okay, so when you met Booze, you knew about him already. You just hadn't actually been introduced to each other?"

"Yeah, I mean he started coming into the Wasabi and I knew him as a customer. Then he and Wesley partnered up, so he was kind of my boss, I guess."

"So, you started dating after he became your boss?"

"Yeah, you're not supposed to date customers," Linda said frowning. "I mean, girls do it, but Wesley doesn't like it."

"Have you ever dated Mel Sharpe?"

"No," Linda screeched as she recoiled back in her chair. "Mel's married to Mabel."

"Okay, so how often do you see Mel and Mabel?"

"I don't know. Booze used to go by the shop sometimes when we were in Paxton. They live over there now, and Mel has a shop, a garage."

"Yes, I know," Conrad said trying to look squarely into Linda's eyes and ignore the sparkle. "I've been there, and I know Booze got some of his medication there."

"What?" Linda's eyes looked down at the table as she sharply shook her head. "No, Mel doesn't have anything to do with that. He and Booze were friends."

"Booze had a specific drug he wanted," Conrad said leaning forward with his forearms resting on the table.

"His doctor didn't prescribe it and so he asked his friends to get it for him. That's not a question. I know that to be true. I also know he picked up the drug at Mel's business when you were there. I'm not accusing Mel of anything and I'm not trying to catch a drug dealer. I'm trying to find out why Booze wanted it. He asked all of his friends to help him, so it only seems logical that he asked you, too. Working at the Wasabi, I'm sure you met a lot of people who could have provided that kind of thing."

Linda took a deep breath and relaxed. "Yeah, I know he was wanting some Zyprexa. I don't know why, but he said his doctor wouldn't give it to him and until he found a new doctor who would listen to him, he wanted to get his hands on some."

"Do you know why? Did he tell you how he thought it would help him? Had he taken it before?" Conrad felt a small crack opening in Linda's story, and he was trying to pry it open.

"He said he had some stuff to clear his mind and it wasn't working anymore. He needed to try something new. The doctor just wanted him to keep taking the same old stuff."

"So, you asked Mel to help him find some and then he started taking it. Did it help him? Could you see any change in him?"

"Booze was always trying to find something, you know. He wanted to feel good and make his problems go away. His wife and all that drama was just too much."

Conrad was pleased to see she didn't dispute his statements and he counted that as progress. "And did this new drug help?"

"I don't think so. I mean, maybe he thought it did, but I didn't see it. Of course, it could be just because he drank too much. I mean, you aren't supposed to drink with stuff like that, right?"

"So, why did you send the drug with Montana over to Tuttle? I mean, you were right there. You could have just given it to Booze yourself."

"Because I didn't want Booze to keep asking me for it, you know. I don't like to get involved in stuff like that. I don't do drugs. That's not my thing."

"Okay. I get it. Did you warn Booze not to drink with the medication? Did you know how many pills a day he took or anything? Without a prescription, how did he know how to use it?"

"He seemed to know. He said he'd read up on it and he needed it. I didn't argue with him about it. I don't know anything about Zyprexa."

"How do you know Montana Black?" Conrad asked abruptly and saw Linda struggle with the change again as her eyes darted around the room.

"He works for Mel. He comes in the Wasabi sometimes, too."

"So, you knew him before Booze?"

Linda stared off into the corner of the room. "Yeah, he dated one of the girls I worked with, but that's all over now."

"So, you first met him at the Wasabi?"

"I'd seen him before, but I'd never talked to him until he started dating Ruby. He started coming out to the Wasabi more to see her and that's when I talked to him."

"But, you're friends now."

"Yeah, I guess." Linda shrugged her shoulders and seemed unsure about how she wanted to answer that.

"You know he's dating Booze's ex-wife?"

"Yeah, I know," Linda said sneering. "He just thinks she's going to get a ton of money from the divorce. I told him that wasn't going to happen."

"You first thought the divorce was finished. When we talked earlier, you told me it was final," Conrad reminded her.

"Yeah, Booze told me it was, but I didn't know then that the judge never signed it. They did have an agreement though, so it was as good as done. Now he's gone and died. It's messed everything up."

"So, you thought you would get everything when you married Booze?"

Linda's posture straightened and she tried to squint her heavy painted eyes at him. "I wasn't trying to take anything from Booze. Not like her. Booze wanted to take care of me. He loved me and we would have been happy." Linda dropped her head and feebly tried to cry without tears.

"How is that any different from what Montana was doing?" When Linda ignored his question, Conrad ignored her fake sorrow. "You both seem like you were in it to get what you could."

"What's wrong with that?" Linda snapped. "I found someone who wanted to take care of me. You think I'm going to walk away from that?"

"So, you took care of him? He wanted some pills and you saw he got them. Right?" Linda's head was down, and Conrad knew she was trying to think things through. "You told him how many to take and what to do to feel better. When he got confused or forgot things, you were there to handle it. And when he was too groggy to drive, you drove him around where he needed to go. You came by the Nutmeg Inn that night and told him to take his pills and rest while you went to work. You thought the divorce was final and he had a new will. You thought everything would be okay. It makes perfect sense." Conrad shrugged as Linda's head rose slowly. "I understand why you did it. I'm not judging you."

"Everything was perfect," Linda said with a strangled choke. Conrad thought her tears might actually be real this time. "Now, everything is ruined. He should have been straight with me. He should have told me he wasn't divorced yet and his wife was going to get the ranch. He should have told me that Stan stole all his money. Booze lied to me about all of that and everything went wrong."

Conrad paused a moment as Linda wallowed in her misfortune. "Well, it's not that you didn't have a good plan, Linda. It just happened too soon. You should have waited until you two were actually married and all." Conrad saw her despair transform into regret as she raised her head slowly and shot her most sorrowful gaze at Conrad. Asher was right. Linda did tend to overact her parts.

"You know," Conrad said standing. "Timing is everything. I'll be right back."

Conrad pulled the interview room door shut behind him and chuckled at his own joke.

Chapter 22

"Chief, Paulie Childers from the Spicetown Star keeps calling. He wants to know if you've made an arrest in the Lockhart death. He says he's already talked to the coroner's office and knows they've got it flagged as a suspicious death. He wants a comment from you for tomorrow's paper." Georgia nodded her head towards interview room one. "Have we got one?"

"Tell Paulie he can talk about the holiday events in tomorrow's paper. I'll give him a statement for Saturday. I'm not ready to show my hand yet." Conrad knew Cora Mae had given Paulie her full speech that wasn't read at the statue dedication and she was secretly hoping the Star would print it and punish the City Council for their actions. Conrad didn't want to muddy up her front page.

"Tuttle's in room two," Georgia said. "He asked if Kathy Lockhart was here. I just told him I didn't know."

"He probably saw her car in the lot. It's the black Mercedes down on the end. She left it here this afternoon when she went to the fair."

"Yeah, I saw her leave a few minutes ago with a young girl. She didn't come in."

"No, we talked this afternoon though. How was Tuttle when he came in?"

"Seemed fine to me," Georgia said shrugging. "Wasn't uptight or angry that I could tell."

"Good." Conrad turned and headed into interview room two.

"Evening, Mr. Tuttle. So glad you could join us."

"Don't you ever work days, Chief?"

"Ah, the job of a Chief of Police is not measured by a clock," Conrad chuckled and smiled.

"I find it very unprofessional of you to constantly demand my presence in the dead of night. I was ready to retire for the day and you send the local police to bang on my door. It's quite unsettling," Tuttle said with an indignant jerk of his head.

Conrad smiled to see the little man was going to start off with the pompous and arrogant show again. He could play that game. "Actually, I wanted you here this afternoon and we tried to reach you by telephone. You might recall I did mention I might need to speak with you again and asked politely that you be available to me. You did not answer our call. I took advantage of the inconvenient delay you caused and enjoyed some of the holiday festivities in town. Now, it's time to get back to work. Where were you today, Mr. Tuttle?"

"I don't have to answer that," Tuttle said as he quickly crossed his legs.

"Oh, I already know, but I wanted to see if you were going to lie to me this time. The last time I asked you where you were the night Booze died, you lied to me. I'm just testing the waters tonight before I dive in."

Tuttle didn't acknowledge Conrad's comment but stared off into the corner of the room where the recorder sat on a tripod with a small blinking red light.

"Oh, you're right," Conrad said as if Tuttle had commented. "I should have started with that. Over in the corner there, you'll see a video recorder. Let me formally advise you that this interview is being recorded for the benefit of the prosecuting attorney's office. They were unable to be present and I didn't want them to miss anything."

Tuttle turned his head quickly away from the camera and gave Conrad an angry glare. "That buffoon who put me in this room already read me my rights. What do you want?"

"Well," Conrad said drawing the word out slowly. "I wanted to give you a chance to tell your side of it all. I realize revenge and greed can take over a man. I've been in law enforcement for many years and seen it happen. Sometimes, you just can't control it."

"What are you talking about?" Tuttle's whole body bristled with agitation and anxiety. He shifted his body away from the recorder and cocked his head sideways. "I've told you everything I know about Booze Lockhart and I'd like to go home."

"Now, there you go, lying to me again. I understand your time is valuable, as is mine, so let's not waste it chasing tales."

"What is it you want to know?" Stanford Tuttle's demeanor softened slightly, and Conrad pushed ahead.

"We've already hashed out the whole scam you were trying to pull on Booze to get your house back, along with whatever money you could funnel off his accounts. Somehow when we talked last though, you forgot to mention the part cousin Linda was playing."

"Linda? If you're talking about Linda Lavender, she was Booze's girlfriend. I'm sure I told you that."

"I'm talking about Linda Sneedman, your gold-digging cousin. You had her buttering up the old guy and getting the groundwork right before you planned to just push old Booze off the proverbial cliff. That was the missing piece for me. It all makes sense now."

"Are you insane?" Tuttle jumped up from his chair and his face began to pale. "Are you actually accusing me of trying to kill Booze Lockhart?

"Not by yourself," Conrad said as he motioned for Tuttle to return to his seat. "I know you're not that good at dealing with other people and you needed some feminine help there. Linda could coo and stroke old Booze into doing almost anything it seems."

"I don't know what you're talking about. This isn't making any sense. What did Linda do?" Tuttle's pasty complexion was beginning to show those telltale pink blotches and Conrad knew he was not far from seeing red.

"Now I don't mean to speak badly of family, but Linda's not very bright and her acting needs work. I'm sure she took some coaching to play the part right."

"Have you talked to Linda? What did she say?" Tuttle had turned around to lean forward against the table.

"Oh, yeah," Conrad said throwing his thumb over his shoulder. "She's right next door. She's answered everything I've asked of her. She's quite easy to talk to and I didn't find her lying to me nearly as often as you have. I admit, the plan had some awkward turns to it. It may have been too complicated for her. I mean, especially since she didn't know you were lying to her, too. She's knows all that now, though."

"I didn't lie to Linda about anything. She just wanted Booze because she thought she'd get money out of it. Women like that are a dime a dozen."

"Yeah, but I think she thought you were helping her, when really it was all about you."

"I did try to help her. She is an idiot and I told her she'd be smart to keep Booze happy. That was my only involvement in their relationship. I don't know what she told you, but that is where it ended."

Conrad saw the first trickle of perspiration slip below Tuttle's hairline and he wanted to see him melt. "Now, put yourself in the judge's shoes. Like you said, it's pretty clear that Linda lacks the capacity to create the sordid web you wove between Kathy, Mel, Montana, and Linda, especially once the forensic accountants tear into your records. Now, who is the judge going to see as the mastermind of all that? Linda? I don't think so."

"I want an attorney," Tuttle said slamming his closed fist on the table and standing.

Conrad jumped up and walked behind Tuttle. "Put your hands behind your back, Mr. Tuttle."

"You're arresting me!" Tuttle's high-pitched squeal caused his body to tremble as Conrad put cuffs around Tuttle's wrists. "I can't stay here. I've got a cat at home. Somebody has to take care of her!"

"We'll get you an attorney once those offices open up in the morning. I'm sure I can get someone at the Red River PD to go check on your cat, if you need them to do that."

"What am I being arrested for? I'm entitled to know. You can't just lock me up."

"I'm holding you on suspicion of conspiracy to commit murder of Beauregard Lockhart Junior, and yes, officially, I do have the right to lock you up based on the statements I've gathered."

"You can't just do this. I'm entitled to a phone call."

"I'll make certain you get your telephone call at a reasonable time. I don't think anyone needs to be called in the middle of the night."

"Did you arrest Linda, too?"

"No, I told you. She's next door," Conrad said as he pushed Tuttle toward the interview room door.

"But she was in on the whole thing. She's the guilty one. She's the one that told Booze to take those pills, not me. I tried to help her."

Conrad reached around Stanford Tuttle and pulled the interview room door open to guide him through.

"Linda," Tuttle yelled. "Linda!"

Wink was waiting on the other side to provide Tuttle escort to the jail and grabbed Tuttle's elbow.

"Well, the way I see it," Conrad said as Tuttle tried to look back at Conrad over his shoulder. "Cousin Linda is mostly guilty of trusting too easily, listening to you, and having really bad timing, but that's for the judge to decide." Tuttle whipped his body from side to side to try to avoid Wink's grasp. "Officer, give Stan his Miranda rights on your way downstairs, will ya? I don't want him to feel neglected."

Conrad turned away as Tuttle yelled unintelligible things at Wink and opened the door to interview room one.

"Miss Sneedman," Conrad said holding out his hand to encourage her to stand. "I believe I'm going to have to keep you overnight in a holding cell. It's rather—"

"Why?" Linda said with a pout as she stood up helplessly. "Was that Stan? Was he yelling for me?"

"Yes, I spoke with your cousin Stanford and he wants an attorney. It's too late tonight for that, so we'll have to work on this further tomorrow."

"But I told you what you wanted to know. I answered your questions."

"Yes, but you see, I asked him about the same things we talked about, and he has a different story. He's indicated that you were the one responsible and until I know for sure, I need to keep you here."

Linda stood up and nodded, but Conrad saw real tears were falling this time and black streaks were forming on her cheeks. That makeup was going to look really scary come morning.

§

"Where is everybody?" Conrad said as he walked through Amanda's outer office and saw her computer glowing, but she wasn't at her desk. Peeking in Cora's office, he waved when he caught Cora's eye.

"Chief, come on in. The Spicers are here. They just dropped in on their way out of town."

Conrad reached out and shook hands with each of them. "Good morning."

"We just wanted to stop in and thank everyone before we left town. We've all had a great time in Spicetown," Mike Spicer said as he squeezed his grandson's shoulder.

"Yeah, it's pretty cool here. I told my dad we should live here since it's our town," Bradley said.

"Well, we'd love to have you," Cora said. "You'll have to bring your folks here and you can give them a tour of everything."

"Oh, they're going to come," Bradley assured her. "I took lots of pictures with my phone, but they've got to see the statue in person. It's super cool. It even kind of looks like my dad."

Ellen Spicer nodded. "It really does."

"I told them we'd send them a copy of the video Rodney took of the dedication," Amanda said.

"Good idea." Cora popped up from her chair and gave each of the Spicers a hug as they departed with waves of thanks and goodbye. Cora saw Rodney waiting in the lobby to say his goodbye, too.

Returning to her office, Cora saw Conrad drop a small white bag on her desk as he sat down in a chair across from her.

"What's this?" Cora studied Conrad's face for an answer. He looked tired and she sensed the stress of the Lockhart death might not have been resolved yet.

"A cinnamon bun from the Fennel Street Bakery. I just came from there," Conrad said holding up his coffee cup. "I thought you might like one."

"You know I love them," Cora said with a twinkle in her eye. "Thank you. Is everything okay? You look tired."

"I got to bed late last night. The coffee will fix that up, though. I've got Linda Lavender and Stanford Tuttle locked up, but the reports aren't done yet." Conrad groaned.

"I know that's not your favorite part."

"No, it's not. On top of everything else, there aren't many people working today. It's really inconvenient having a holiday on a Thursday this year. Everybody takes Friday off and I have to scramble to get anything done. There're only two attorneys working in the prosecutor's office today. Tuttle is screaming for an attorney and I can't even rustle up a defense for him. It would have been easier on me if I'd waited until this holiday was over."

"You have enough to hold them, right?"

"Yes, they're so busy ratting each other out, it should be an easy case. Alice called this morning and has finalized her report. The coroner's report shows cause of death as a heart attack from drug overdose.

"I got another nice piece of evidence this morning from the State Crime Lab. They've got print matches on that key from the Nutmeg Inn. One of the matches is a guy in Montana's motorcycle club. I'm pretty sure Tuttle probably sent Montana over there to try to grab Nellie's camera or film. The other print belongs to Linda Lavender."

"Do you have to go back to Paxton to get the motorcycle guy?"

"No. I just put in for an arrest warrant and the Paxton PD can pick him up. I'm sure he'll roll over on Tuttle and help seal up that end."

"So, there wasn't a second will, was there?" Cora said as she pulled out the sticky bun and put it on a napkin.

"No, I talked to Tuttle's brother, who did the first one. He said Booze called him about changing the will, but he advised him to wait until the divorce decree was final. He didn't know anything about Linda Lavender, though. He said Booze just wanted his wife cut out of the will and his daughter put in her place. I guess Booze lied to Linda about all that. I didn't find any evidence that indicated Booze planned to marry her. This was just a case where everybody lied to everybody else."

"What's funny to me," Cora said, pausing to wipe off her fingers before reaching for her coffee cup. "People who lie to everyone, seem to think other people aren't like that. They know they're lying, but they think everyone else is telling them the truth."

"That certainly happened in this case," Conrad said as he took a swig from his cup.

"Well, you are who you associate with," Cora Mae said, wagging a schoolteacher index finger at Conrad. "I always told my students to choose their friends carefully and, in this case, one liar finds another."

"That's why I hang around with you," Conrad said chuckling. "It makes me look good."

"Well," Cora Mae said fluffing her copper hair with the palm of her hand. "Somebody has to be the pillars of the community around here."

Conrad's laughter made him spill his coffee on his shirt as Cora Mae giggled and raised her cinnamon bun in the air.

∞

Sheri Richey

★ The Spicetown Star ★

FOUNDER HONORED ON 4th

-- On Thursday, Mayor Cora Mae Bingham unveiled the new statue located in front of City Hall honoring the founder of Spicetown, John Spicer, following the 4th of July parade.

John Spicer and his family had established a home here in the late 1800s, inviting family and friends to join them in the development. When the United States Postal Service began regular mail delivery by railway, John Spicer requested a stop for his community, which they labeled "Spicer Town". John Spicer met the train and hung the mail bag for pickup each day for the citizens of the community.

As the community grew, the members voted to choose an official town name and in 1881, selected Spicetown, in honor of John Spicer and his family.

Although the mayor kept her dedication speech brief due to the excessive heat of day, she did introduce the descendants of John Spicer, who were town guests for the day's events. The statue was paid for by a historical grant the mayor secured independently when the City Council failed to support her mission.

(See page 3 for additional photos and to read the Mayor's full dedication speech.)

Sheri Richey

Next in The Spicetown Mystery Series

Blue Collar Bluff

I'd love to hear from you!

Find me on Facebook, Goodreads, Twitter, my website or join my email list for upcoming news!

www.SheriRichey.com

Sheri Richey

CPSIA information can be obtained
at www.ICGtesting.com
Printed in the USA
LVHW032219180522
719074LV00009B/1001